Death in the New Land

Kaye George

A People of the Wind Mystery
Book 3

White City

Press

Also by Kaye George

A People of the Wind Mystery

Book 1
Death in the Time of Ice

Book 2
Death on the Trek

Death in the New Land

Kaye George

This edition published by White City Press
An imprint of Misti Media LLC
https://www.mistimedia.com
Available in both Paperback and eBook Editions
1 2 3 4 5 6 7 8 9 10
Copyright © Kaye George 2024
Paperback ISBN: 9781963479232
eBook ISBN: 9781963479133

Acknowledgements

One of the best parts of working on these prehistory books has been the interest others have shown, and the kindness of them in sharing discoveries they come across that they know could be helpful to me. It's a long list! I hope I haven't left anyone out.

Here goes. Much gratitude to:

Marilyn Levinson for help with the basic plot.

Cathy Getz for thinking of ancient man finding dinosaur bones and making up dragons.

Elaine Douts for an article on interbreeding.

Nancy Raven Smith for an update on the migration path down the Pacific coast.

Marilyn Johnston aka cj petterson for an early genetics article, also for the article on grinding up grains in the Americas before there were any oats.

Sheri Gormley for an article on grinding.

Douglas DigDug Taylor from the Prehistoric Writers and Readers Campfire group for Tucumcari research and information.

Bobbi Groth for articles on possible early Neanderthals in America.

Jessica Morgan for an article on the Denisovan tooth.

Jan Christensen for general plotting and editing help.

And many other fans of the series who have given me encouragement and support along the way. I believe I used all of the above contributions in this work and they made it so much better.

I also extend my heartfelt thanks to Jay Hartman. The suggestions, editing and support has been terrific throughout this series.

Author's Notes

If you haven't read the first two novels in this series, *Death in the Time of Ice* and *Death on the Trek*, I think you'll enjoy this story without reading them first (but you should also read them, of course). Just in case this is your first encounter with this series, I want to give you some background you might need.

TIME: This tale takes place about thirty thousand years ago, near the end of the existence of Neanderthals (*Homo neanderthalensis*) as a discrete population, just as the last great Ice Age was beginning over the whole globe.

SETTING: There is no evidence Neanderthals were in what is now North America, but there's no evidence they weren't, right? I selfishly took artistic license to use NA as a setting because I'm in love with the mega fauna of that time and place.

PEOPLE: Back then, many different kinds of people were on the planet at the same time. They weren't all in the same place, but I have gathered them together to be my characters. What used to be called Cro-Magnons and are now called early modern humans (but were different than modern *Homo sapiens*—much taller, for instance) are called Tall Ones in this text. Denisovans are called Hoodens. The Red Deer People are mentioned, but not seen. Reference here is made to people in a previous volume called Mikino. Those are my version of the small *Homo floresiensis* (also called Hobbit people), who lived in Java. Other Neanderthal tribes are called "people who look like" them in this series.

Read on, and enjoy your trip to an era we'll never thoroughly know, but are learning more about every day.

Chapter 1

Enga Dancing Flower didn't know when she had been so happy. Certainly not since the trek to this New Land began. The long, hard journey had started at the end of the last Cold Season. Her tribe, the Hamapa, was a group that numbered the amount of all toes and fingers, plus a few more. They almost wholly depended on the large herds of mammoth to survive. That was because they ate the flesh, treated the hides to make dwellings and clothing, and weighted those dwellings with the huge tusks.

But, when a Great Ice formed and moved toward them, all vegetation in its path was destroyed. The mammoth seemed to understand this and, little by little, they moved away. Soon there were not enough to sustain the Hamapa and they were forced to follow the herds to a place more warm where they all could dwell. Staying where they were would have meant certain death for all of them.

On the way to this New Land, where they now dwelled, she and her tribe had known much danger and fear. Feelings of dread had lasted for many moons, until the very recent days. As she did every time she felt that she could allow her mind to wander, she had given thought to the baby she had carried inside her body on the journey, and had lost, and to the life that the child might have had. Even though they had encountered many dangers in this place, she, and her whole tribe, must now trust that they would be able to survive here. To grow their tribe here. To thrive here.

Now, at dark time, the tribe gathered around their new fire pit, the Elders sitting content with the work of the day, the musicians getting ready, the children playing at the edges of the gathering. Their high, light voices sounded like music to the ears of Enga Dancing Flower.

Ung Strong Arm, the birth sister of Enga, sent her a thought. *It appears that Dakadaga, the Spirit of Mother Sky, smiles on us at this dark time.*

Enga thought-spoke back to her, agreeing. *She is gazing at us with so many eyes. Does she have more eyes in this place than she did in our old home?*

Maybe. Look! There is one that is falling.

They both gazed at the bright streak that ran across Mother Sky.

I think that is a good omen, Ung thought-spoke.

The village they had set up when they arrived here was situated near the banks of a stream, deep enough to be a challenge to cross when it was running fast. A vast forest spread behind them. It was a source of nuts and berries in their seasons, and it felt protective. However, they had not explored it into its depths, so did not know everything that it held. The land on the other side of the stream was flat, dotted with pine trees, and only interrupted by an odd-looking mountain, which they had not explored thoroughly. Much remained to be discovered here.

It was still the hot season, which lasted a long time in this new place. Some of the heat left the air after Sister Sun left the sky, though. The dark times were cool and refreshing.

They dressed in their usual mammoth skin coverings. Some slung bear or rabbit skin capes over their shoulders against the relative chill of the evening. The capes were more soft than the heavy mammoth hides. Most of the females wore their hair in braids. Some of the males tied theirs up in topknots, or gathered it behind, at their necks. The firelight caught expectation in many eyes. All looked forward to the gatherings at dark time.

When a wave of something hostile flicked across the mind of Enga, she straightened her back and focused her thoughts on it. But it was gone before she could concentrate enough to intercept and interpret it. She sniffed the night air. The only odors she detected were the slightly smoky fire, the succulent meat they had just eaten, the fresh pine scent of the nearby forest, and the warm comfortable smells of her tribemates. Lifting her shoulders and giving her head a small shake, she decided she had only sensed some animals out prowling at night. There were many animals in this place that she knew nothing about. None of her tribe did. They had followed the mammoth, the animals they knew, and were glad that they were here with them.

Enga glanced over at little Sooka and felt something leap for joy inside her. The female child had not started out as her own, but she was completely hers now. Sooka helped her to not think about the child she had lost, not quite so often nor quite so deeply. Sooka had been born with the seed of a Tall One, not a Hamapa, so she was not the same as all the other babies. She had grown tall more quickly, and had always been more active. She had not walked at an early age, compared to Whim, a typical Hamapa baby who was born at about the same time Sooka was. The skin of the Hamapa tribe was light, some of them were freckled, but the skin of Sooka was even more delicate and the rays of Sister Sun made blisters on it if she was uncovered for too long. When she was in the open, the tribe made sure her limbs were covered and not bare.

The Hamapa birth mother of Sooka, Vala Golden Hair, had been banished from the tribe after attempting to slay Enga, with the help of Bodd Blow Striker, who had been mating with Vala after he and his tribal brother joined the Hamapas from another tribe. Enga did not care to think about those things now. Vala had been the cause of much anger and sorrow, but she was gone. Those bad times were over and Enga never wanted to relive them. Vala and Bodd were gone. She flung them from her mind.

Her own mate, Tog Flint Shaper, sent her a thought from where he stood, on the other side of the circle gathering. *Sooka will make a good Hamapa. For some time I did not know if she would ever fit into our tribe.*

Enga admitted, *I also wondered if she would. I do know at this time that she will, and she does. She is ours now and I have much love for her.*

I do also.

Enga smiled into his dark eyes. She knew he liked the dimples her smile created, and warm feelings passed between them. He also loved her long hair, the color of flaming fire, and her eyes, which were almost the sky-blue of the large, wide eyes of baby Sooka.

The banished ones, Vala and Bodd, intruded into her thoughts, but she firmly put them out of her mind again at this happy dark time and turned her eyes to Brother Moon. He had awakened and was peeking around that high place that lay a short journey away, on the other side of the small stream. The water of the stream flowed gently, making faint, soft shushing sounds along the banks. It provided a constant rippling backdrop to all of the other sounds in this place. The stream was not large compared to the rivers they had crossed on the way here, but the water was more deep at this place. It bore a faint scent of fish and water plants.

Tog Flint Shaper, her mate, walked toward her from where he had been conversing with two other males. His dark eyes never failed to draw her in. He turned them to her now, but her own eyes were, as always, drawn to his strong, broad chest. The bone he used to secure his topknot had been carved by her and she loved to see it there. Now she felt the warmth of him as he sat on the ground beside her, while they waited for the dancing to begin. Fall Cape Maker tooted a few sweet notes on his flute. Sannum Straight Hair thumped a tentative rhythm with the palms of his hands on his hollow low, then started a familiar pattern, one of the several he used. Fall caught the beat and sent accompanying notes into the night air from the wooden flute that had belonged to Panan, the former flute player, who was now deceased. Lakala Rippling Water stood and soon began to sing a Song of Thanks for the new undertaking they would start at new sun. They were soon to have a shared feast with another tribe of beings who looked like the Hamapa and lived nearby.

Ung Strong Arm, intercepted the thoughts of Enga and sent her own back, intruding. Their thoughts were closer than most, since they were birth sisters.

My Enga, it is a good thing we will have new people to trade with, as we had in the Old Land.

The thought stream was sent in a wave of dark colors to shield it from the other tribe members and make it private.

I know it is a good thing. But I still wonder what they will be like. Will we find new, close friends there, or just trading partners? I wonder about this.

Ung answered. *There are some Hamapa who need mates. It is hoped by me that they will want the same thing from us. It is good to get mates from many places.*

Little Whim, the only other very young child in the tribe, toddled past where Enga sat with Tog. He was about the same age as Sooka, but had developed as all Hamapa babies develop, walking many moons before Sooka had, and he had a placid, easy temperament. The two children were very different but liked being together and playing together. Now, he stopped to look at the smoke rising into the sky, then walked toward it, not looking at where he was going. His foot caught on a stone that surrounded the fire pit. When he stumbled, Enga sprang up and grabbed him to keep him from falling into the fire.

His mother, Fee Long Thrower, was beside them as quickly as a flash of lightning. *Thank you, Enga Dancing Flower. I was not watching him. It was just for such a short time.*

It is easy to lose track of these babies. It is good we have a whole tribe to help. Enga smiled at Fee, who was now clutching her baby son, and returning to where she had been sitting, stroking the soft, light hair of the child and cooing to him.

He was unsettled after almost falling into the fire. Enga, and the whole tribe, felt he would be more careful now. And they would all be more watchful than they usually were. The children of the tribe were most important. They were the future of the Hamapa.

The music grew more insistent, more loud. The heart of Enga quickened, as it always did at this time. Soon, Enga and Ung, along with the many others of the tribe, rose and began dancing in a circle around the fire, so as to help the sung words of Lakala reach upward to Dakadaga, the Spirit of Mother Sky with their motions. It was important that Mother Sky, who was always above and watching, be appeased. She was the most high Spirit among the many that they appealed to and attempted to appease. Her wrath could be terrible, and the tribe needed her breath to be gentle, not fierce, and her tears to fall softly and not make the nearby stream overflow to flood their new settlement.

A second blessing was also sung for the meeting with the Yamapa tribe tomorrow, the first official meeting with these newly discovered neighbors. In the place where they had dwelt for many, many summers, they had often traveled in warm seasons to trade dried meat, knapped flint, treated skins, and any objects they had in abundance for those they were lacking. These were times of joy also, seeing people who were known, but were seldom seen. Feasting and dancing were always part of those short journeys. But the Hamapa did not know the ways of the tribes who lived here. Did all peoples have the same customs? Would they welcome trading days? At least the Yamapa tribe said that they welcomed the joint feast.

The tribe members who now danced wore their finery over their everyday mammoth-skin garments. Enga still had a soft rabbit skin cape that had made the journey. Tog flung the tails of his dire wolf cape in his gyrations. The eyes of Enga drank in his strong back and handsome face.

Even while dancing and thinking other thoughts, Enga now caught part of a stream of thought-speak between her mate, Tog and a few other males. They were discussing a bridge over the stream as they circled the fire.

Yes, we should have a way to cross the water, came from Tog. *We need to decide how to construct it.*

Some discussion followed about how to do that.

Enga thought that would be a most excellent project. They often wanted to go onto the other side of the stream and at times had to travel a distance to get to a place shallow enough to ford. Behind the place where they were making the new village was a vast coniferous forest. The mammoth roamed on the plains, dotted with clusters of pine trees, on the other side of the stream, so the water had to be crossed for the hunt.

Jeek let some of his private thoughts stray and Enga could tell he was communicating with young Gunda, the birth child of the present Hama. A small smile crept onto the face of Enga. She very much liked both Jeek and Gunda, young ones of thirteen and eleven summers, the numbers of all fingers and one toe or three toes. Maybe someday they would mate. That would be a good thing for the tribe.

Cabat the Thick sent a public thought to Akkal the Burmana, the Firetender, *The fire you built is good at this dark time.*

Enga, and everyone else, could see the pride in his thought-speak, glowing with a shimmering hue, like the white light from the eyes of Mother Sky.

Akkal sent an answering thought to Cabat, who was his birth father, *We will soon need to find a place to store the flames. A place where the fire can be sheltered and saved so it will not go out when Mother Sky sends her teardrops to Brother Earth. A safe, dry place.* Cabat the Thick and Akkal Firetender had always had a close relationship.

The tribe very much missed the Holy Cave that had been left behind. They needed to find a new one for their fire, and for other purposes. Losing the fire could be a disaster for them. For now, they could only hope that a fierce downpour of tears from Mother Sky would not drown out this one and leave them without a means to cook and to get warm and dry. That would be needed soon, when Cold Season came upon them.

The mountain they could see in the distance from here, the one Brother Moon had now risen above, might have such a cave for them. There was an urgent need to explore. Many in the tribe sent thoughts of agreement with Akkal.

For now, there was much to dance for, much supplication to be made, and Enga shook her head and flung her braided hair, threw her arms as she twirled, and leapt with her feet moving quickly in her agile movements. The tribe sent approval to her. As the most skilled dancer, it was her duty to always do her best so the Spirits would notice and would be kind to the tribe.

Pausing in her dance movements, she quickly reached into her waist pouch and drew out the carved wooden figure that looked like Aja Hama, the leader who was now departed. Aja Hama, *Former Most High Female*, had been a person very dear to Enga while she had been alive. She had welcomed Enga and her sister Ung Strong Arm into the tribe when they were orphaned as children from another tribe. Enga wanted to always keep her memory fresh and alive, for her and for everyone. Enga set the figure at the edge of the fire, far enough away so that it would not burn, but where the tribe would see it and dance around it. Maybe the spirit of Aja Hama would notice and would bless the tribe. She was not a real spirit, not like Mother Sky or Brother Moon, Sister Sun or Brother Earth, but the mind of Enga thought of her that way.

A bit of scorn made its way to the mind of Enga. She knew it came from Cabat the Thick. He did not want Enga to revere the figure of Aja Hama. He had once, long ago, been the mate of the Hama, when she was still alive, but they had parted sometime after Akkal Firetender had been born to them. Cabat thought Enga was foolish for putting so much importance into a carved figure of the leader who was now dead. He sent as much praise for the fire as he did disdain for the carved figure. Enga clamped her mind closed to the scorn, threw her shoulders back, and continued sending her best dancing into the night.

It was only when retiring for the rest of the dark time to one of the two big new communal wipitis, that she again caught a wave of hostile thought. The hairs on the back of her neck stirred. The thought was much worse than the light scorn from Cabat. This time she was able to pause and get a better sense of the origin. This was not from an animal who wished them harm. This was from a person who wished them harm.

Chapter 2

Some 10,000 Neanderthal artifacts, hearths, and a sleeping area have been found this month at Abric Romaní, an archaeological site in the Catalonia region of Spain. Archaeologists from The Catalan Institute of Human Paleoecology and Social Evolution (IPHES) found a hole among the hearths and heated rocks near a wall of the rockshelter that may have been used to heat water some 60,000 years ago. Other artifacts from this level of the cave suggests (sic) that the Neanderthal inhabitants used different parts of the cave for butchering game, tool knapping, and trash disposal.
—https://www.archaeology.org/news/3642-150827-hot-water-hole, August 27, 2015

Sister Sun was halfway finished with her journey across Mother Sky and the Hamapa were halfway through their visit. The two tribes were meeting at the village of the Yamapa. They had laid out the bounty each group brought to the feast, and had partaken of it in friendship. Jeek thought this was a lot like the gatherings with the other tribes that they used to have in the Old Land. Except those had been much more large, with many tribes traveling to share food, tools and other things to trade.

The mind of Jeek pondered this new tribe, in relation to his own. His tribe, the Hamapa, called themselves the *Most High People*, which was "Hamapa" in their spoken language. They spoke seldom, but had standard, common words for many things when they did. This new tribe engaged in thought-speak very much like the Hamapa and had told them they were the Yamapa, the *Most Good People*. They were somewhat strange. Instead of one *Most High Female* as their leader, they had two, called Yama and Yama Doe. That would be *Most Good Female. Females*. Such an odd people.

They all had brought fresh mammoth meat that had been roasted over their own fires before coming together for this gathering. The Yamapa also had strange meats that the tribe of Jeek had never tasted. They did not know what these animals were from the names given by the Yamapa. The way the meats smelled was odd to them. They were not bad smells, but new ones.

Jeek ducked his head as one of the young Yamapa females approached him. The deerskin she wore clung to her body when she moved and her loose hair swung when she walked, long and lustrous. She was not the first one who had come to him to talk, but she was the first one who made a strange thumping happen in his chest, a thumping that grew fast and loud. His skin turned the color of Sister Sun when she wore her brightest clothing at the end of day. He did not want to talk to the pretty Yamapa females. He did not want Gunda to think that he would like to know them better. He only wanted to know Gunda better. Not anyone else. He did not even know what to say. The mind of Jeek grew soft and slow as she approached.

A thought came from Enga, a private one, wrapped in a soft blue color.

Young Jeek, I do not think Gunda would be upset if you thought-spoke with this female. If you look across the central village space, you will see that Gunda is surrounded by young Yamapa males. This is a time to have fun and to get to know these people. It is just for this day.

He realized that, once again, he had let his thoughts leak to Enga. Jeek gazed across the central place, a space of hard sand rather than paving stones as the Hamapa had used in the old village. Those stones had been laid a long time before anyone now living. Maybe someday they could have a paved stone place again in this land.

He saw that Gunda was, just as Enga said, surrounded by a few of the strong-looking young males from this tribe, their hair flowing down their broad backs. They all looked more old than Gunda and him. He wanted to run over there and grab her away, but Enga saw that thought also and told him to not do that. *Talk to this young female. We can all be friendly to each other. We want this tribe to like all of us.*

Those were wise words, Jeek knew, so he turned his face to the female and stretched his mouth into what he hoped was a smile, even if it was a stiff one.

I am called Ranga, the young female told him. *What are you called?*

Jeek told her his name, explaining why he only had one, plain name. *I have not yet had my Passage Ceremony. Have you had yours?* He immediately felt stupid. If she had an adult name, she would have given it to him. Of course she had not had her ceremony. He knew that she, like him, has not yet lived for the time of fifteen summers. He could tell she was not quite that old.

I have not, but I think about it. I want to be Ranga Dark Eyes when that happens.

Jeek gazed at her eyes. They were indeed dark. So dark. They were as dark as Mother Sky was when all of her many bright, twinkling eyes were hidden by thick cloud garments. They were also deep, like a pool of fresh water in a dark cave. When he realized there was a foolish-looking grin on his face, he looked at his feet instead. It was a great effort to not glance over at Gunda, to see if she was observing what a fool he was being.

Do you know what your name will be? She ducked her head to see his face. *When you have your Passage Ceremony? Have you picked one?*

He jerked his head up to face her. Was she treating him like a young child? *Of course I know.* He had known for a long time. His birth brother had been given the title Teek Pathfinder for a time, but it had been changed to Teek Bearclaw after an attack by a bear left deep scars on his back. *I want to be known as Jeek Pathfinder.* He knew he could use the name, since his brother no longer used it.

Pathfinder! Are you good at tracking? Can you trace where animals and people have been? Do you use their scents?

He wasn't sure if he was good at that or not. In that moment, he realized, for the first time, that maybe he did not want to be called Pathfinder. He had never given it much thought. It had been another stupid thing to tell her. He had long been trying to learn to spear, on the hunt, as the females did. Males had never done that, but he wanted to, and was becoming more skilled all the time. He would probably better be named Jeek Spear Thrower. Of course, he would not be the one picking his name. Hama, their leader, would do that. So what he wanted did not matter. His words to Ranga were so foolish. But he did not want to express all of this to her.

He shrugged at Ranga and looked away. She left him to talk to Mootak Big Heart who sat with his two small birth brothers and Akkal Firetender. They all jumped up and greeted Ranga with smiles. To Jeek, the smiles looked as goofy as the one he had given her. They also thought she was the most pretty of the young Yamapa females, he could tell.

The elders of both tribes clustered together. Jeek noticed the new neighbors trying to describe some of the creatures they hunted for food and for their hides. One seemed like a large cat, more large than the cat of long tooth they had known in their Old Land. The young female describing it told them it had spots on its hide.

Hama grew excited. She sent a thought to her tribe. *We know this animal. We have seen it on our long trek.* Then she broadcast a picture to everyone of the jaguars they had seen when they encountered the small people in the Mikino tribe. Those small people had not treated the Hamapa well on their journey. They had kept jaguars cruelly imprisoned in caves and did not treat them well either.

Mootak Big Heart, the Storyteller, nodded. He remembered the Saga that had been handed down to him, of the time, long ago, when the Hamapa hunted them and wore their pelts. Those animals had long ago left the Old Land and remained only in stories handed down by Storytellers.

Many of the Hamapa nodded their heads. No wonder the small, cruel people kept the cats captive. The meat tasted at least as good as a juicy, fat piece of mammoth flesh.

The Hamapa grew excited to learn that this tasty animal, which no longer lived in their Old Land, was here, in the new one. They nodded to each other. All the meats were succulent and delicious. In addition to the meats, they were served a new type of food. These were fleshy plants that had been cooked, but not over a fire. Jeek could tell that because there was no taste of fire or smoke. He was too busy enjoying the taste and the texture to ask about it. The food felt different in his mouth. It was fleshy, but soft and easy to chew.

The Yamapa did not wear thick mammoth skins like the Hamapa did. Their clothing was thin, maybe some kind of deer skin, Jeek thought. They also wore their hair in a different manner. Instead of the braids that many of the Hamapa wore, most of them caught their hair in a leather thong at the backs of their necks. Maybe, Jeek thought, his own tribe could wear ceremonial clothing that was not so heavy, so that they would not be so hot in the fierce rays that Sister Sun gave off in this place. His tribe wore lightweight lion skins and loincloths for hunting in hot weather, but not for occasions like this one, a feast with another tribe, even when it was very warm. Right now, mammoth skins were the most formal garments they had. The skin of Jeek grew wet and slick under Sister Sun in his heavy garment. He knew that was happening to his tribemates as well.

As with other tribes of their own kind, they were all able to read the thoughts each person sent out. They all had similar ways to cloak their thoughts, also. When the thoughts rode on bright, brilliant colors, everyone could receive them. They each used their own special dark colors to send private thoughts to another individual. Jeek wished that all people, all kinds of people, could do this. But he knew that they could not.

Not wanting to see if anyone was behaving as foolishly as he had, he roamed around the village, to avoid others and to see what this village was like.

Their dwellings were similar to those of his tribe, but there was one structure that was different. It consisted of skins stretched on poles to form a roof. The skins reached toward the ground, but did not go down all the way, only about half the distance. He could not resist ducking down to take a peek inside. There, he found many small stone fire pits, arranged in a circle. The small fires in them crackled and glowed. They were spaced so a person could easily walk between them to the center, where there was another pit, larger and lined with stones. He ducked under the half wall and crept inside to see what was in the central pit. It was round, about as far across as two or three Hamapa hands, and it was half full of water. That is, he thought it was water. It did not lie still as water did, but bubbled. It was extremely hot inside the structure.

When Ranga came up behind him, he almost yelped. Had she gotten bored with Mootak and his brothers so soon? Should he feel so good about that?

She smiled and he was held captive by those dark eyes once more.

Why are you in here? she asked.

I wanted to know what this is. Why is that water bubbling? Is it hot?

Yes. This is where we heat our water for cooking.

Cooking? With no fire? With water? How do you do that?

She showed him some mental pictures of a person taking a stone that had been heated at the edge of one of the small fires and dropping it into the water, causing the water to steam and bubble. She picked up a hot rock, protecting her hand with the hem of her deerskin garment, and tossed it into the water where it hissed and sank, sending up a plume of steam.

We can use hot water to cook grains and tubers and sometimes to cook meat when it is very tough.

Jeek was astounded. This tribe was very clever. He realized that the food that did not taste of fire and smoke must have been cooked this way.

A sound of loud voices came from the gathering of adult males near the edge of the central space. The voices were full of anger. Jeek ran out of the structure and heard Tog Flint Shaper shout aloud.

The Hamapa used thought-speak almost all the time, except for official Pronouncements at important times. Jeek was shocked to hear this verbalizing.

"Nasa nasa nasa," Tog yelled. *No, no, no.*

His face was angry. He stood with his nose and his toes nearly touching those of a large, strong Yamapa male who was a bit more tall than Tog.

Jeek ran to them quickly to see what was happening. What could be causing such a commotion and such hostility?

When he reached the group, he was almost thrown back by the strong smell. It did not smell like something to eat or drink. It smelled like something that had rotted. The males had been drinking something from gourd cups. One of them lay before him, tipped over and spilling its liquid contents in a puddle. He stepped in it before he realized it was there. That is where the smell was coming from. From this liquid that the males had been drinking. It was not water.

Tog flung angry thoughts at the male he faced. The faces of both of them were twisted and ugly. *My knives are far better than any you could ever make. Do not tell me how wonderful your knives are.*

That is what I am telling you. You cannot tell me what to think. Or what to tell you, or anyone else. You could never make a knife like mine. What do you know of knives? What do you know of anything?

Jeek could smell the same foul odor on the breath of the two angry men. This was not a good thing and it frightened him. Once more, his heart was beating too fast, but this was for a bad reason.

When the two local female tribe leaders, Yama and Yama Doe ran into the group and pulled the men apart, Jeek let out a breath he did not know he had been holding.

*****

Enga Dancing Flower had been watching the males drinking the liquid where they sat, in a group away from everyone else. She had wanted to ask someone what they were doing. And what they were drinking. She did not think it was something that they were enjoying. The more they drank, the more quarrelsome and belligerent they became. Why did they keep drinking it, she wondered.

When her mate, Tog Flint Shaper, jumped up to confront the large Yamapa male, shouting hostile words, she felt prickles of alarm inside. And also outside, running up her back. She could see into the mind of Tog. It was cloudy and confused. And he was angry at the other male, but she could not tell why. His mind was more murky than she had ever known it to be. She felt like she did when a mammoth was charging toward her in panic and she had to be alert and react. There was danger here.

As she jumped up to try to intervene, the two village tribal leaders stepped in and drew them apart. Enga could not tell which leader was which, as they looked so similar. One of the Yamas clasped the head of her own tribal brother to her chest and stroked his head. The other Yama held Tog from behind as he struggled to break free from her. Several of the other males who had been drinking together put themselves between the two. When Tog saw this, he quit struggling, but the anger stayed, blazing in his eyes.

Enga had reached him by this time. The Yama released him and Enga took his hand, always hard and calloused, but now limp in hers, and she led him away. She did not think she could converse with him about this until the fog left his mind. She did not know how long that would take. But she knew the fog was from the drink they had been sharing. The more he drank, the more that fog had clouded his mind.

One of the other Elders from the Yamapa tribe followed them. Enga bade Tog sit with her in the place where she had been. It was slightly removed from anyone else. She had been conversing with two of the Yamapa adult females, but they were not there anymore.

The Elder, a male with a crippled and bent arm, stood near them.

Do you think you will be alright? Do you need any assistance? he asked.

I do not know, Enga answered. *Will Tog Fling Shaper be all right? What were they drinking? Is it the cause of the clouds in the mind of Tog?*

Yes, I am sure it is. He will not feel well. The liquid is the juice of fruits and berries. The juice sits a long time in a container and gets strong. It is called old juice. He has drunk too much of it. Do your people not drink this for special occasions?

Enga asked him what he meant.

He described how his tribe gathered ripe fruits, and a few berries, squeezed the juice out of them and put that mixture into a skin pouch, to keep for a long time, until the juice smelled strong.

The taste is bitter, but also sweet, he said. *We do not drink this often. We save it for important times. It does make our heads foggy, but it also gives us pleasant feelings. That is why we drink it. It is good not to drink too much, but the young ones do drink too much sometimes.*

She shook her head. She had never heard of such a thing.

He continued. *Maybe the juice is too strong for your male. If he has never had it, it is like he is a young one. They must be instructed when they first drink it.*

Enga looked at the face of Tog to see what he thought about this. She could tell he was not able to think clearly yet. *Will the fog leave his mind?*

The Elder assured her that it would, but that it might take all of the dark time to do so.

Enga decided that this old juice was not a good thing to drink.

Chapter 3

Soon after the altercation between Tog Flint Shaper and the Yamapa male, the Hamapa tribe decided to leave. Hama stood to give a parting Pronouncement.

"Hoody! Hama vav," she said aloud.

Enga was glad to see this. Putting an official ending on this gathering was a good idea. They all heard the words in their heads. *Listen! The Most High Female speaks.*

"Hamamapapa ta Yamampapa. Tata yaya. Hamamapapa poos wa wipiti."

The Hama tribe thanks the Yamapa people. The food was good. The Hamapa go to our own dwellings.

Many from both tribes nodded their heads to agree. It was time for the gathering to end. The faces of all were solemn in the flickering firelight. Mother Sky had sent a gentle puff of breath to cool everyone and to set the flames of the fire pit into a slow dance.

Hama finished her talk in the usual way. "Dakadaga sheesh Hamamapapa."

The Spirit of Mother Sky, bless the Hamapa.

Then she added this, "Dakadaga sheesh Yamamapapa."

The Spirit of Mother Sky, bless the Yamapa.

The members of the other tribe nodded once more to show their thanks and approval.

The Hamapa were soon on their way, carrying a few gifts of feathers and small pelts from their neighbors, leaving behind the tantalizing cooking smells that almost made some of them want to stay longer. Some of the males who had been drinking the old juice had trouble walking and the females had to prop them up. The journey was not long and they were glad of that. However, as they neared the place to wade across the stream, Hapa, the Elder who was the mate of Hama, stumbled going down the embankment and fell onto his face into the water with a loud, watery splash.

Then they all heard the voice of Hapa, groaning.

This was not a good thing. Elders were dignified. They did not stumble and fall. But Hapa had also drunk the old juice.

Enga could discern Tog waking from his fog slightly in reaction, and thinking about the need for the water crossing that they had been discussing. Even with his face in the water, Hapa sent out an agreement with Tog that everyone could read. There was a great need for a crossing over this water.

Enga thought there was also a need for new behavior the next time these two tribes got together. But she kept that to herself.

Back in the village, Akkal quickly got a large fire going so Hapa could squat near it to warm and dry himself.

The village had been constructed over the last several moons, since their arrival, and now consisted of a central place of trampled dirt and two large wipitis of treated mammoth skins laid over upright mammoth tusks set firmly into the ground. There was also a smaller structure where Hama and Hapa slept, and where private meetings with them could take place.

The tribe had hunted many times to collect enough tusks and hides to construct these first dwellings, which would serve to shelter them during the Cold Season. When that season was over, they would collect many more tusks and skins, taking more time to cure them in a better way, and they would construct separate dwellings where each pair of mates, some with their young ones, would live. As in the old place, there would be two larger ones for single males and for single females.

Eventually, one of the large ones they had already built would be the dwelling of Hama and Hapa. The leaders needed extra space to hold meetings of the Elders and others. The small one was considered adequate for now, though.

Enga was surprised when Tog shook her steadying hand off his arm and ran into the woods, heading to the place where the tribe relieved themselves. She heard him bring the feast up, spewing it from his mouth in a foul-smelling stream. She ran after him and steadied him, then brought him back and rinsed his face off with water from one of the gourds near the fire.

All during their sleeping time, Tog made many loud noises with his nose and throat. Sooka awoke two times because of the disturbance.

At new sun, when everyone gathered for a morning meal, the males who had drunk the old juice all looked sick. The skin on their faces was pale and seemed to be tinged with a faint green color. Some held their heads with their hands. Some made soft moaning noises. Tog told Enga that it felt like rocks were pounding together inside his head. She tried not to laugh, but the way he looked amused her.

Please tell me you will never drink old juice again, she thought-spoke to him.

He shook his head slightly. Then clutched his head in both hands and moaned again, but softly. Enga hoped that he would remember this feeling and would not drink it again.

*****

Jeek was excited. Two whole days of exciting new things were about to take place. At last sun, they had had the feast and meeting. At this sun, there would be target practice. These practices had not been happening as regularly as they used to before the big move, but Fee Long Thrower had sent out a message to all the young females—and to Jeek—that she wanted them to practice throwing their spears more often in the coming days.

Fee led them to the place she had set up in the woods behind the village. It was on the same side of the stream, so they did not have to cross it. Jeek was glad about the location. He did not like wading through the water, even when they went downstream where it was more shallow.

The old gray wolf skin they had used for spear practice for so long had gotten too tattered, so Fee had managed to get a piece of camel skin that was not being used for anything else. She had picked a new location for practice. The place they used last time had been too near the water and some spears had gone into the stream. Now they were a bit deeper into the woods, in a place where there was a natural clearing. It seemed ideal for their practice.

The females lined up and, one at a time, flung their small spears at the skin, which Fee had stretched between two saplings and fastened with strips that had been torn at the corners of the target skin.

Gunda and her two birth sisters, Pala and Mulee, were directly in front of Jeek. He was the last to take his turn. Ever since he had started joining them, it had been done this way. He did not mind. He enjoyed watching the others. But mostly he enjoyed watching Gunda. When her turn was finished, she swiveled her head and he could see her eyes, the color of leaves in the springtime. She smiled and he stepped up to take his turn.

His spear hit the center of the skin, as it almost always did. He had practiced alone in the woods for a long time, throwing a stick at berries on the bush, before he made his wishes to be a spear thrower known. Now, he was as good as the best of the young females with the target. Fee Long Thrower had been letting him carry a spear on their hunts for many moons now and he was so happy about that.

He had thought, at first, that he was doing this to impress Gunda, but knew now that he was not. He was throwing a spear because he loved throwing a spear. Bringing down an animal for the tribe was the most high honor he could think of. Maybe he could do that soon.

*****

After the rising and the setting of a few more suns, when all the males were recovered from the visit to the Yamapa, it was decided to have a hunt. The Elders had decided they should bring home more building materials to use for more dwellings after the Cold Season was over. If they had these things in the village during the long, dark, coming days, they could start to work on them. They could use more meat, too. Then they could dry and smoke what they did not eat and they would have ample meals for many moons. They always had to make preparation for the Cold Season, no matter where they lived.

Jeek could not hold back a grin at this news, which had been given in a group thought by Hama at the evening gathering around the fire. Fee Long Thrower had told him he was to go on this hunt as a spear thrower, and not just to carry them. He was so happy about this he had trouble sleeping in the dark time before the hunt.

The task of the males was always, until now, to follow, to help corral the beasts if that was needed, and to cut up and carry home the animals they were able to slay. Females were the only ones who threw spears and brought down the prey, since they had more patience than males. This meant that they could also work on spear throwing until they could hit the targets almost all of the time, and they could also lie quietly long periods, waiting until the animals approached close enough to hit. The males were stronger, so it was right that they carried the prey home. Sometimes the distance was long. They used skins to drag the prey—the meat and the bones and tusks and hides—and it was a job that took much strength. It was good that the distance to where the animals took water was not as great here as it had been in the Old Land.

Jeek once again wondered why he wanted to hunt with the females, but he knew that it felt right for him to do so. He had worked so hard, practicing a lot over a long period of time, in the Old Land and in this one, and he was ready for this hunt. He tried hard to sleep so he would be rested and ready, but woke often during the dark time, which seemed to last extra long, thinking about the hunt with a stirring inside him of excitement.

Sister Sun greeted them with warmth and wore only a few wispy garments. There was no sign that Mother Sky would shed tears that day.

After they had eaten, Hama gave a Pronouncement for the hunt.

"Hoody! Yaya, Hama vav. Dy, Hamamapapa tza tiki dunk. Dakadaga sheesh Hamamapapa. Leela sheesh Hamamapapa."

Listen! Yes, the Most High Female speaks. This day, Hamapa slay the large beast. The spirit of the sky, Dakadaga, bless the Hamapa. The spirit of the hunt, Leela, bless the Hamapa.

Bahg Swiftfeet and two others had gone on a scouting trip at last sun and found a herd of mammoth at the watering place near the village of the Yamapa. The hunting party would travel there today to bring home one of them.

At high sun they all got together. The tribe made a circle around the fire pit, full of glowing embers now, and chanted together, "Leela tza sheesh. Dakadaga tza sheesh," hoping the two Spirits would *bless the kill.*

Enga and the other females picked up the spears lying on the ground, the spears they had danced around the night before. The males made sure their flint knives were in the pouches which hung from their loincloths and they threw the large hunting skins over their shoulders. With those, they would drag back the fruits of the hunt. As always, two males and the Elders stayed behind with the smallest children to guard their dwellings. Cabat the Thick and Akkal Firetender held Sooka and the male baby of Fee Long Thrower, Whim. Enga waved her spear at Sooka and the child smiled and waved her arms in the air to answer the goodbye.

The hunt was starting!

In the Old Land, they had to have the habit of setting out very early for the watering hole, but here, where it was not so far, they could wait until high sun. They wanted to be in a good position as the light of Sister Sun was starting to fade.

Trotting across the flat land, through the clumps of pine trees and scrub, they soon drew near the lake, where dense clumps of small trees grew near the water. The hunters spread out, as was their custom, the females, the ones who would throw the spears, hid in the undergrowth.

They had not known if there would be material to cover their body odors, so they had carried fragrant pine boughs with them. Each person clutched one close to the body to mask and confuse the scent, as much as possible.

Now they would wait, silent and unmoving, until Sister Sun approached Brother Earth, ready to eventually disappear inside him. At that time, when the light was growing dim, when the breath of Mother Sky usually grew still, the animals would come to take water.

The tribal brothers and the older children would wait farther back in a thick bunch of trees, until it was time for the kill to begin. Then they would have their own tasks also. If the animals stampeded and the males were needed to guide the path of the animals as they ran, they could jump out and do that.

As they crouched, waiting for the moment to strike, Ung Strong Arm sent a thought to her birth sister, Enga. *Is this land much more hot than the Old Land? Was Sister Sun ever this fierce during this season?*

I think she was not. I wonder if she will remain this way during Cold Season. Enga was glad of the thought stream to distract her from the tension she always felt at this part of the hunt. The fragrance of the pine boughs was strong, but they would be able to smell the animals when they approached if the wind was right. She silently, privately, implored Mother Sky to send her breath in the right direction to help the Hamapa. The sweat of Enga ran down her face, dripped between her breasts, and made her palms slick. She wiped them often on her garment.

We must ask some others, ones who are always here, how the Cold Season will be.

But, thought-spoke Enga, *they are always here. They would not know if this place is more hot or more cold than a place they have never been to.*

Ung sent her agreement to that thought.

As Sister Sun sent many brilliant hot-colored rays into Mother Sky behind them, and Brother Moon appeared as a slim sliver, wearing a few wispy white garments, the eyes of Mother Sky began to pop into view. Even though they were far from their old home, and so much was so different here, the eyes of Mother Sky were in the places they were accustomed to seeing them. It gave the whole tribe comfort. As in their old home at this time of the day, Sister Sun seemed to steal the colors from everything and take them with her as she disappeared. The fresh green of the pine needles, the brown of the dirt beneath them, the blue of the water—they all began to lose their own colors, and all became the same dull shade in that time before everything turned black for the night.

The buzz of insects and the trill of songbirds had grown more and more quiet. The animals who hunted in the dark time had not yet begun roaming. The air grew still. Mother Sky was barely breathing.

Enga heard Ung draw in a deep breath. She did the same. Yes. The night breath of Mother Sky was now stirring a bit and was sending them the heavy, pungent scent of mammoth. That meant that their own scent was blowing away from the herd. It was a relief that the Spirits were being so kind. The animals would not detect them unless the direction of the air changed.

They waited. The beasts ushered their most small ones into the water where they splashed and played, pulling the water into their long noses and spraying it at each other. Some of them pushed air through those long noses into the water and made bubbling sounds. The larger ones, the females and the males who were not yet adult, plodded to the edge to slurp water with much noise. Mammoth herds were led by a female, as the Hamapa were. A large young female stayed behind, standing guard.

Some mammoth herds in the Old Land had included a few camels, but there were none with this group.

In their position, the huntresses saw the herd spread out before them, the small ones to one side, playing in the water, the large one guarding on the opposite side, the rest ranged between them, all in a row. This hunt would not be difficult. They should be able to bypass the large guardian without much trouble.

Ung Strong Arm, the leader of this hunt, sent a message to those hiding in the woods near the water, asking them to distract the guard elephant. Soon a few of the older Hamapa children emerged, slowly so they would not scare away the rest of the herd. They crept out, crouched low, wagging their heads from side to side.

The mammoth guardian concentrated exclusively on the strange movements of the Hamapa children, beings who could potentially harm her herd, while the huntresses ran, quick and quiet, to pick off the most small adult female near the water.

The spear of Ung hit the animal in her eye, the best place for a spear to land. The animal opened her mouth wide and screamed through her nose. The spear of Fee Long Thrower caught her in the open mouth and she fell with a thud that shook the ground.

Enga Dancing Flower and Ongu Small One saw that they were not needed for this animal and ran toward one of the larger adolescent males. Both threw their spears into his head.

As the rest of the herd stampeded away, the Hamapa males, waving their arms and shouting, made certain they fled in the direction they had come from, away from the rest of the hunting party. Everyone helped put a few more spears in both animals so they could make certain that neither of the animals had any life left in them. It would not be good for one to rise up and hurt someone after they thought it had been slain.

Enga noticed Jeek finishing spearing the smaller one. She could tell he was disappointed he had not been able to bring one down by himself. She sent him a thought. *You are young. You can bring down a beast someday. I had to go on many hunts before I brought one down.*

He looked at her and she could tell she had made him feel better. His face relaxed and he drove one more blow into the hindquarters of the animal.

With the breath gone from both of the beasts, they all sat for a short time slowing their own breathing and letting the thumping in their chests subside. The hands of Enga trembled at first, as they always did. But there was a wide smile on her face. She looked around. Every face held a huge smile. Even the face of Jeek. He gave her a special grin.

They had brought down two animals. Two! The female had nice large tusks, and the young male already had tusks also. Not as large, but they would be able to use those in a structure of some sort. The two hides would make clothing and, next warm season, covering for one or two new small private dwellings.

Ung sent a message to the ones left behind in the village, telling them that the hunt had been successful and they would soon return with meat, skin and tusks. First, though, there was a lot of meat to chop into pieces so they could carry it. It might be difficult to bring everything back, but they would do it.

Happy, excited, satisfied thoughts flew back and forth, all of them public. Then Enga caught a wave that did not belong with the rest of the tribe. Soon all heads were turned toward the thick forest, the place where the foreign thought came from. That forest extended onward for a long distance. They could not see where it ended.

A male stepped out from the pine trees. It was a male they all knew. It was Bodd Blow Striker, who had been banished from the Hamapa tribe with Vala Golden Hair after they had both tried to slay Enga.

All exchanges of thought shut down and every muscle tensed on every body.

Chapter 4

Bodd Blow Striker approached them slowly, his head down, while they got to their feet. The females gripped their spears, some of them even crouching a bit, in a defensive stance. The males puffed out their chests and hostility radiated from them. Jeek grew nervous, seeing his tribemates tensed for what might happen. Even the incessant background of birdsong ceased. The air felt brittle. Jeek could tell that he was not the only one startled to see him. He, like most of his tribe, assumed that Bodd was likely to be dead by this time.

Jeek was surprised that Bodd did not look thin, or even sick. He thought that Bodd had probably been living without a tribe, since he and Vala had been banished from this tribe and was forbidden to return to the Hamapa. Banishment almost always meant death, even though the outcasts were given a knife to take with them when they left. But he was still alive. Jeek could not understand how this could be.

Bodd drew his knife from his waist pouch and Jeek felt prickles of alarm rising high, rushing through the minds of everyone. Some of the males set their feet apart and reached for their own knives. The females picked up their spears. Everyone faced him as he approached, muscles tight, minds closed.

May I come forward? Bodd asked. *I mean no harm. I want to help you butcher the animals.*

Why do you desire to do that? Ung asked. *You are not Hamapa now. You can not approach us. Go back where you were.*

I cannot.

Almost everyone shot the next thoughts at him, including Jeek, *Why? Why not? Where were you? Where have you been?*

Can I explain?

Ung took a step forward. *Stay where you are and tell us what you want to say. Do not approach. Do not come near.*

Bodd nodded and sat on the ground. Jeek wondered if this was going to be a long story. Some of the Hamapa sat also, but many remained standing and alert, some with knives still in their hands.

I was betrayed by Vala Golden Hair. She is not as I thought she was.

How did you think she was? Enga asked. She knew that Vala could fool many males with her beguiling ways. She had nearly stolen Tog away from Enga.

I thought she would…I thought we would look out for each other. We were cast out together and I thought we would work together as a team. I thought we would help each other to survive.

Enga received that thought and agreed with it. Jeek received the thoughts of Enga. She could tell he was confused. *You know that it was not usual that these two were cast out together. At all other times, banishment is solitary and is a certain death sentence. Maybe we should not be so surprised that he is still alive, since they left together. But where is Vala Golden Hair now? She is not with him. Is she?*

Jeek wondered the same things, keeping the questions to himself.

Everyone waited for Bodd to continue. His breath came fast and his hands trembled. Jeek thought that he must be afraid of them. He seemed to be waiting for answering thoughts, but, when none came to him, he continued.

We survived by joining a tribe.

Much surprise was expressed by everyone.

What tribe? Fee Long Thrower asked. *The Yamapa?*

No, not a tribe of people like us. A tribe of Tall Ones.

Now, much more surprise came from everyone. Jeek did not think that Bodd and Vala would be able to communicate with Tall Ones.

Where is this tribe? Fee asked.

Bodd Blow Striker and Fall Cape Maker had come to the Hamapa tribe at the beginning of the long trek that the Hamapa had made from the old village at the edge of the approaching glacier, many moons ago. Their own tribe, the Gata, had starved and were dead, all but those two males, who were then weak and most thin. The Hamapa had taken them in. The two were beings who needed help and the Hamapa helped them. That was always their way. The two had joined the tribe and everything had worked out until the end of the trek. That was when Vala had captured the attention of Bodd and tried to use him for her own evil.

Now those two had been living with a tribe of Tall Ones?

They are located not far from here. There is also another tribe across the stream, near where your new village is.

Jeek had met those Tall Ones. He remembered much about them. They wore hides of bison and spoke with odd sounds. They were also led by a male, which was strange. They had given a gift to Hama, a gift of shells strung on a strand of sinew. After that one meeting, he had not seen those Tall Ones again. They had come from the forest and vanished back into it.

So they took you in? You and Vala Golden Hair, thought-spoke Fee. *That is how you have survived?*

That is how we survived. The Tall Ones were kind to us and fed us and gave us shelter.

Birdsong was heard again now and the tension in the air had faded away. There were still many questions, though. Jeek knew that Sooka, the child Enga and Tog were taking care of, who was really the birth daughter of Vala Golden Hair, had come from the seed of a Tall One that had lived with the tribe for a time.

Why are you here now? Jeek could not contain his curiosity. He hoped Bodd was not going to try to reclaim Sooka, the child of Vala. Was he here to trick them and do that?

Bodd took in a large breath and looked to Mother Sky. He then blew out that breath toward Brother Earth before he answered them. *Vala Golden Hair made the Tall Ones believe that I harmed her. The males all like her very much. They cast me out after she made them believe that.*

Maybe Vala could communicate with them better, since she had once mated with one. Jeek sensed some relaxing of tension in many of the minds of his tribe. They had been looking for Vala to appear, and bracing for that, but now they understood that she would not. That would have been much worse than seeing Bodd appear.

My brother, Fall Cape Maker, can you accept me back into the tribe? Bodd looked toward his tribal brother, the one who had come from the decimated Gata tribe with him. There was pain on the face of Bodd.

Jeek saw pain on the face of Fall also. They seemed to be exchanging some private thoughts. Both held their faces very still. There was no expression on either one. Their thought exchange was held between them just as tightly.

Ung intervened. *It is not the decision of Fall Cape Maker. Accepting you back would be the decision of the whole tribe, with the Elders leading us.*

Bodd nodded his understanding. Fall looked at Ung and did the same thing.

May my brother travel back with us? Fall asked. *So he will not be alone while we make the decision?*

I will work, Bodd thought-spoke. *I can help with this task.* He spread his arms toward the dead beasts.

They could use his help, Jeek knew. A few of the adults communicated, with their thoughts closed off from the rest.

Ung sat nodding at the exchanges, then sent a thought to everyone. *Bodd Blow Striker, you may help with this kill and come back with us. We will hold a council at new sun with our leaders. It is there we will decide your fate.*

Bodd was as good as his word and worked alongside his former tribe until all the usable parts of the animals were ready to be dragged home.

On the trip back, Jeek grasped an edge of the weighty skin that held two of the tusks and helped pull it. He stayed alert, though, expecting Vala Golden Hair to appear, no matter that Bodd did not seem to think she would. He felt that everyone was watching for her, not just him. It would not be a good thing if she appeared. She had done much harm to the tribe and would never be welcomed back. Jeek wondered if Bodd would be allowed to rejoin them. The reasons he had been banished were good ones and they had not changed. But, Jeek thought, maybe Bodd Blow Striker had changed. He now seemed like the person he was when he first joined them and was so grateful that the tribe had saved the lives of him and Fall Cape Maker.

It was almost dark and they were almost there when Jeek saw a shadowy figure standing in their path. He grew tense. Was this Vala Golden Hair? It was hard to see without Sister Sun.

Chapter 5

In the growing darkness, Enga Dancing Flower could see that the one who was blocking their path did not have the height of a Tall One. At first she thought she was seeing Tikihoo, the Hooden who had been with the tribe on the trek. The Hooden were about as tall as this person. But Tikihoo was dead. This could not be Tikihoo.

As they drew more close, it was apparent that this was a female. Her clothing looked like it was made of the skins of peccaries, unlike the other Hooden tribe they had met on their travels. Her garment was a tunic, tied at the waist with peccary tails strung together to make a belt. Those other Hooden people had caged giant sloths, and had eaten them and wore their pelts. This one had neither shells nor feathers in her hair, as those others had.

"Tee hoo," the female said aloud, just like a Tall One. She pointed to herself, then gestured toward the big hill.

The Hamapa had called Tikihoo that name because she was large. "Tiki hoo," in their oral language meant "large one." The name had also fit her because her tribe made a lot of sounds like "hoo." Her people were called Hoodens by the Hamapa because of their sounds.

When this person said those words aloud, Enga got a wobbly feeling inside. This could not be Tikihoo. Those words must mean something very different to this Hooden female.

The female gestured to herself, putting her fist on her chest, then opening her palm and extending it toward them with a questioning look on her face.

Enga pointed to the female and then to the hill, making a shooing motion, trying to tell her that she should go back there. Maybe she was saying the word for that place? It seemed to be where she was from, since she pointed there. But Enga saw her shake her head and scrunch her eyes shut, her whole body shaking. There were tears in her eyes when she opened them.

Bodd Blow Striker stepped forward and took her hand. She threw her arms around him, making terrible moaning sounds with her sobbing now. Bodd was a large, sturdy male, but this Hooden was even more tall than he was, like Tikihoo had been. She had the same large, very white teeth, dark skin, and short dark hair that clung to her head. Enga wished she could know what had happened to this Hooden, why she was in this place and all alone, but Enga could tell it was something bad. Maybe she had been cast out of her tribe.

Bodd Blow Striker told them what he had heard from the Tall Ones, through Vala. *There is a tribe of Hooden not far from here. This female must have come from there.*

Why is she here, with us? Enga asked.

That is impossible to find out. She either ran away or was cast out.

Enga considered the situation for a few moments. This Hooden did not look dangerous or violent. Instead, she looked frightened. Enga did not think she would harm them. And she was alone, and wanted to be with them for now. They must continue, back to the village, with the products from the hunt. They could not delay here.

A quick conferral was made and everyone agreed she could stay with them for now.

Everyone started moving on and the Hooden came with them, staying near Bodd as he helped drag one of the heavy-laden skins.

Enga had a thought. "Tikidoe," she said aloud. She smiled at the Hooden and pointed to her. "Tikidoe," she repeated. "Doe" meant the amount of two, so this was a second large (tiki) one, *Tikidoe*. Enga received thoughts of approval from some of the others. She had chosen a good name for this lone female. Now she would see if the Elders would agree on the name, or to her staying with them. Enga did not know why they would object to that. They would be more likely to object to taking Bodd back into their midst than this sad, harmless-looking person.

Ung sent a message to those who had stayed behind in the village, telling them that they were drawing near with much meat and tusks. She did not mention the Hooden or Bodd.

Ung Strong Arm, my birth sister, thought-spoke Enga, *why do you not tell them we are bringing a Hooden with us?*

It may be that they will not accept her. It is better to just bring her. We cannot turn her out at dark time. I did not mention Bodd Blow Striker either. It might not be good to tell them this until we get there.

Enga considered this and thought that maybe her sister was right. There had been many bad feelings toward the other one, Tikihoo, for some time after she joined them, though Enga knew she had not deserved any of that.

Tendrils of welcome reached out to the returning hunt party, bringing smiles to their faces. By the time they reached the village, darkness was nearly complete, but Akkal had created a large, crackling fire, they were all pleased to see. Cabat the Thick stood to greet them and clapped his sturdy hand on the shoulder of his birth brother, Sannum Straight Hair. Sannum was also happy to see the hunters returning. He sent his thoughts out to his mate, Ongu Small One, that he was glad they were all back unharmed. Sometimes things went wrong on a hunt and there were injuries.

The hunt party dropped their burdens to receive a greeting. All of the tasks, chopping the meat into smaller pieces so they could start eating it and, soon, smoking it, starting to treat the hides, and cleaning off the tusks, would be done at new sun. Now, the Elders, the Most High Female and the Most High Male, Hama and Hapa, greeted each person as they filed past them to a place by the fire. Enga stayed back with Bodd and Tikidoe. The ones who were welcoming them home now had not noticed those because of the darkness outside the circle of light shed by the spitting, leaping flames. At last, everyone else had been greeted. The Hama rattled her gourd, giving off a happy sound, and the Hapa and Storyteller nodded at each brother and sister.

Then Enga stepped forward, into the circle of light cast by the fire, holding the hand of Tikidoe. Sooka ran to Enga and wrapped her arms around the legs of Enga. A ripple filled with surprised thoughts went around the group.

This Hooden needs shelter, Enga thought-spoke.

Hama took a step back as they approached. Surprise and suspicion lifted her eyebrows and narrowed her eyes. *Why does she need that?* Hama asked. *Why is she not with her own people?*

I am not certain, but I think she has been cast out of her tribe. We think her tribe lives in the shadow of the great hill.

Why do you think that? Hama continued to look concerned. She was not welcoming the Hooden.

This one is distressed. I tried to point and tell her to go back there, but she shed water from her eyes. I would like to call her Tikidoe.

The Hooden gave a faint smile to the Elders, but her eyes were wide and frightened, and her hand trembled in the hand of Enga. Enga could feel how frightened she was and squeezed her hand for reassurance.

Hama bowed her head in thought for a short moment, then replied. *We will let her stay for a time. We will give her a trial period. We will take a vote later, when we know more about her. It may be that she was cast out for a good reason. The Hamapa may have to cast her out also.*

But you will let her stay for now?

Hama nodded. Then Hapa looked past Enga and Tikidoe, seeing Bodd for the first time. Hapa stepped forward with a heavy stomp. The ripple of emotion coming from most of them was shock, then anger.

This cannot be! This is a banished one, Hapa called out to their scrambling minds.

Can we let him tell us his story? Then decide what to do? Enga did not know why she was trying to convince them to let him stay. Maybe because he was now an enemy of Vala. A person who was the enemy of

Vala was a person who was also a friend of Enga.

The first thing to be done was to eat. The hunters were famished from their long day and their hard work. All sat and ate from the stores of the last hunt before this one. Meat was plentiful at this time and everyone had their fill. Enga chewed some of the meat and put it in the mouth of Sooka, who did not have enough teeth for chewing yet.

After eating, and passing around a gourd full of water from the stream, Hama stood. She nodded at Bodd Blow Striker and sent him a public message.

Enga Dancing Flower wants you to tell us what has happened to you. We will decide whether or not there is a reason to let you stay here.

All eyes turned to him. The thoughts ranged from tentative to wary to distrustful to angry. Many held their breath, waiting to learn what he would tell them.

Tikidoe sat between Bodd and Enga, who cradled Sooka. Sooka dozed with a full, fat tummy, her chubby thumb in her small mouth. Tikidoe had eaten as much as anyone else and seemed content. And was still wary, on guard. Enga was glad she would be allowed to stay for now and patted the back of her hand. Tikidoe gave her a shy smile. Enga wished she could tell Tikidoe what was going on.

The high-pitched scream of a rabbit being caught by a night predator split the silence.

Bodd stood to plead with them. *When I was taken in by the Hamapa, I was grateful. Fall Cape Maker and I would have starved without you, as the rest of the Gata, our tribe, had done. I am still grateful for that, for you. I always will be. When I met Vala Golden Hair, she entered my mind. She soon took over. She started controlling my thoughts and not letting me have my own thoughts. I could not form any ideas. After we were both cast out, I began to free myself from her, but it took a long time. I could only do it for a little while during each sun time. At dark time, I would lose my own thoughts again. Then I would have to start over at the next new sun. We were taken in by a tribe of Tall Ones not far from here.*

But you have left Vala, Hama thought-spoke. *She is not here. How did that happen?*

Two things happened. First, I became strong enough to control my own thoughts when she left my mind. That happened because Vala Golden Hair became attached to one of the Tall Ones and left my mind on its own for long stretches of time.

Many strong thoughts floated through the tribe, thoughts of remembering how Vala had mated with a Tall One. A Tall One who planted the seed of Sooka in her. Beneath these thoughts were veiled ones, thinking that something was wrong with Vala, that she was not right, not a proper Hamapa, for her to want to mate with a Tall One. Not everyone shared that thought. Enga did not, and several others. Enga did agree that something was wrong with Vala. She was not right, but mating with a Tall One did not make a person wrong acting. Any of the Hamapa could have done that. And others had, in the past. The wrongs of Vala were far more than that, to the mind of Enga, and to some of the others.

Enga stayed alert to the thoughts of Bodd. He was tuning into the obvious emotions of the tribe, which were being sent out among themselves, all seated in a circle around the fire. He could also almost make out the low rumblings below the open thoughts, Enga felt.

He continued. *Then another thing happened. She began to tell the Tall Ones untrue things about me. I do not know why she did that. I was glad to have her leave me alone and be with the Tall One. But she was not satisfied with that situation. She wanted me to leave. So she told them that I pushed a child into the water. And that I cut the leg of an old male with a sharp stone. Vala did these things. I told them that, but they did not believe me. They all believed Vala.*

So you were banished from the tribe of the Tall Ones, Hama thought-spoke.

Bodd let his head drop forward, onto his chest. *Yes, they banished me.*

Enga had to ask him a question. *How did you find us? How did you know to come to us?*

I did not. I did not know you would be there, so close to where I was. I had not gone very far after being cast out. I hoped to be able to go back to them. They had been so kind at first. And I had nowhere else to go. So I stayed near to them. But when I detected the Hamapa on the hunt, I was glad. I picked up your scent and some of your thoughts. Being with the Hamapa is better than being with the Tall Ones. And much better than being with Vala.

The Elders exchanged quick, brief thoughts as the others sent ripples of murmuring, indistinct emotions to each other. Then Hama stood. She nodded at Bodd. Dismissed, he crouched down beside Tikidoe. The Hooden reached for him and Enga saw him take her hand in his.

Hama sent out her thoughts. *Bodd Blow Striker will stay with us or he will go. We will decide together. If you wish for Bodd to stay here, stand on this side of me.* She spread her arm to one side of herself. *If you wish for Bodd to be banished again, stand on this side.* This time she spread her other arm to her other side.

The tribe members turned their heads, watching one another, still seated, each one waiting for someone else to make the first move. The thoughts of all were shrouded in dark colors so that each person guarded each thought and nothing escaped to the others. Enga felt someone stir. Her mate, Tog Flint Shaper, rose and stood on the side which meant he wanted Bodd to stay. Enga was glad to see that. It is what she wanted to do also, but had not wanted to be the first one to do this. She scrambled up, holding the baby, and walked over to stand beside him. One by one, the Hamapa got to their feet and chose a side. Enga was glad to see many of them joining her and Tog. In the end, Cabat the Thick and his seed, Akkal Firetender, were the only ones on the other side.

Enga saw the defiant look on the fleshy face of Cabat. He would have to accept Bodd as a tribal brother. No matter if he did not want him back. It was the decision of the tribe. She knew that Akkal would do whatever Cabat did.

Tikidoe, puzzled about what was happening, had gotten up, but had not known where to go. So she stood beside Bodd, who was facing Hama and the ones who had judged him.

Hama nodded at both sides. *It is decided. Welcome back, Bodd Blow Striker. We have only three wipitis at this time, until next warm season when we will build more. You will stay with the males.* She added, *Tikidoe will stay with the females for now.*

It was true, mostly males were in one dwelling and mostly females in the other. But some couples also slept together in both places. The children also slept both places, with their birth parents. Hama had not bothered to mention all of the details of their temporary arrangements to Bodd.

Enga knew that Tikidoe could not understand thought-speak. *I will show Tikidoe where to sleep when it is time,* she thought-spoke to the tribe. She would let Tikidoe lie near her and Tog and Sooka. Someone would have to guide Bodd when it was time to retire. Or maybe he would just figure it out.

One more nod of thanks from Hama, and it was time to have music, singing and dancing. This was always the best part of any day for Enga, even after a strenuous hunt. She looked upward and could see, mixed with the smoke rising from the cheery fire, the comforting many eyes of Mother Sky, watching over them. The breath of Mother Sky again felt more cool at dark time. Maybe they would need to wear capes for the evening gatherings soon. She would have to find one, or make one, for Tikidoe. Sooka also needed a new one for cold weather.

Soon, there was noise and laughter, music and dancing. So why did Hama and Hapa look at each other like that? Like they were afraid of something?

Then Enga felt it, too. Several beings were approaching. They did not smell like tribes who looked like the Hamapa.

Chapter 6

Denisovans… We don't know what they looked like, what kind of communities they built, how tall they grew, how they hunted, how they treated their dead… Though it's difficult to extrapolate much from a tooth, this new one's unusual size affirms one of the only things we do know about the Denisovans: they were large.

—"DNA sheds light on mysterious, big-tooth human relatives," by Sarah Kaplan, November 17, 2015, *The Washington Post*

They appeared at the edges of the light cast by the village fire. They were people who were more tall than the Hamapa. They were as tall as Tikidoe, and Jeek knew, from the way they looked and dressed, that they were Hooden, like her. Two of them stepped forward and there were only a few more behind them.

When Tikidoe saw them she looked afraid. She dashed behind Bodd Blow Striker, clutching his body. Bodd patted the arm and shoulder of Tikidoe and stayed where he was standing, on the opposite side of the circle from the intruders. Jeek was glad Bodd was defending her. Despite her size, she seemed defenseless to him.

Hama and Hapa stepped forward to confront the visitors. They were joined by Hava, the Storyteller. Then Akkal rushed to join them. Cabat the Thick, who had not been dancing, rose with a noisy grunt, and walked to stand with them. Then the Healer, Zhoo of Still Waters, and Fee Long Thrower joined them. They all made a barrier between the Hooden and Tikidoe.

Jeek was not the only one who sensed a threat in their arrival, in the stern expressions on their faces, and in their wide-legged stances.

The male who seemed to be the leader of the Hooden made gestures with his hands, while speaking their odd language. He wore a crown of woven grasses, as had the other Hooden leader they had met. His companion only had a large feather stuck into his hair. Maybe the crown was a symbol for his position as an Elder and a leader.

"Hoohoo noonoo," he spoke, pointing to Tikidoe and shaking his head. "Teehoo," he said, pointing to her and off in the direction of their own village, by the high hill. He repeated this last word several times, always with the same gestures.

Hama bent over and picked up her long stick. It had been her spear when she had been younger and had hunted, but now the spearhead was not on the end of it and she sometimes used it for a walking stick. She planted one end on the ground and gripped it, her eyes narrowed and her lips thin. The rest of the tribe followed her example and picked up their spears from where they lay, if they could reach them, the spears having been scattered here and there after they had returned from the hunt. Those not standing in the front line brought spears to those who did stand there.

The line of his tribemates with their weapons looked daunting to Jeek. He hoped the Hoodens also looked at them that way.

The Hooden leader shook his head side to side and held his hands out, palms upward. He was not holding a weapon, though a knife was stuck in his belt. He pointed to Tikidoe again, then touched his chest with his palm. The look on his face was one of pain, Jeek thought. His lips were pulled back in a grimace, his huge teeth gleaming in the firelight. It was clear that he very much wanted Tikidoe to come back with them. It was just as clear, however, that she wanted to stay with the Hamapa. Maybe that was even more clear.

46

Finally, after the standoff had gone on with no one moving forward or backward for more time, enough time for the fire to start burning down, the Hooden leader shook his head with sadness. "Noo," he said, wailing, and they all turned and walked away with slow, heavy steps.

Jeek let out a light breath of relief, although the number of the Hooden had been only the same as the number of fingers on a hand, plus one more. There were many more Hamapa.

Everyone stared at Tikidoe. When she noticed that she was the center of attention, she started making verbal noises first to Bodd, and then to everyone, using hand gestures.

First, she pointed at the place where the intruders had stood. She walked to where the leader had been and pointed to that space and to her. Then she joined her hands.

Jeek wondered if she was telling them they had been mates. Bodd nodded at her and broadcast that he also thought that was what she was saying.

She reached up under her loose garment, put her hands to the place where babies come out of a female, and acted like she was catching something, then like she was cradling a baby to her breast. She looked around, pointed at Whim, then made the cradling motions again, keeping a pinched look of pain on her face.

Bodd thought she had given birth to a baby with that leader. The rest agreed. What she was communicating seemed plain to them.

Tikidoe made more cradling motions, then pointed with one hand to the place where a baby would be, on her other arm, if she were cradling one. Then she pointed to her own foot. She turned her foot inward so that it was at an odd angle. Several times, she pointed to her foot and the place where the baby was, in the minds of everyone.

What happened next alarmed Jeek. She threw the imaginary baby to the ground and stomped on it.

This alarmed Bodd, along with everyone else. He pointed to her, asking her with his thoughts that she could not receive, *Did you kill your baby? Did you hurt your baby?* As he did that, he began to point at her and to the ground where the imaginary baby had been crushed.

She shook her head, pointing to herself, then pointed where the leader had gone and associated him with the crushed baby.

The Hamapa concluded that the leader had killed her baby. They did not know for certain that this had been done, but it was the only thing they could interpret from her actions. The baby must have had a deformed foot and the leader did not want a tribal member with a deformity. That did not seem right to the Hamapa. It was a very wrong thing. Their minds grew cold, thinking of a person who could slay a baby. And his own baby, it seemed.

No wonder she does not want to go back with them, Bodd thought-spoke. He gathered her in his arms and clasped her while she shed many tears.

After several moments of silence, except for the weeping of Tikidoe, Akkal built the fire back up and dancing eventually continued, but with less joy and enthusiasm than before.

*****

At first sun, Bodd Blow Striker awoke to find everyone gone from the wipiti where he had slept, even Tikidoe, who had curled up next to him at some point during dark time. For these past few dark times, he had not been able to fall asleep for a long time, then would sleep so soundly near first sun, that he would not feel ready to awaken for the day. His fear of Vala Golden Hair was the reason for his wakefulness. He was almost certain that she would not care that he was gone, but he was not completely certain. If she bore ill will toward him, she might want him dead. He had trouble relaxing and more trouble falling asleep.

This day, he pushed the door flap aside and entered the common central space. He was greeted by the smell of the mammoth meat from the last hunt being smoked. The parts of the animal which were not smoked had mostly been eaten. They all hoped they would be able to process enough to get them through the Cold Season when it came. The strips, cut from the loins and the shoulders, hung on a rack near the fire, catching the smoke to preserve it. As long as they were there, a guard had to sit with the pieces of meat, until they were done and could be stored inside as jerky, away from hungry animals.

The central place was nearly deserted. Where was everyone? Tikidoe sat near the fire pit, across from the drying rack, weaving grasses together. He wondered what she was making, so he sat near her to watch, crossing his legs like she did.

She gave him a shy smile and picked up a piece of meat from the small pile she had been consuming. When she handed it to him, he realized that everyone had already eaten. He took it, thanking her with a nod, also realizing how very late he had slept. He looked to the sky to see that Sister Sun was nearly overhead.

Hama emerged from the small dwelling she shared with Hapa.

Where have they gone? Who is left here? he asked.

They are on a hunt. Some of them wanted to wait for you, but they decided to go ahead when you did not awaken. Others were impatient to try to spear some small game before they go to wait for the mammoths at the watering place.

Bodd wondered who had wanted to wait for him. Those were probably his allies. He knew there were those who did not want to accept him back. He suspected there were more than just Cabat and Akkal, though they had not stood with those two.

Tikidoe was tilting her head at him, trying to understand what he was doing, carrying on a silent communication that she could not detect. He turned his attention to her, chewing the piece of meat and watching her hands. Her large fingers flew and a shape began to form. Then he remembered how the Hooden leader had worn a crown of woven grass when they had come to try to take her back to their tribe.

He pointed to her project and raised his eyebrows. He had been successful in conveying his meaning, which was to ask what she was doing. She gave him a big smile and pointed at his head. He could tell now that it was going to be a crown, as he had guessed. She set it, half-finished, on top of his head, to show him. Then she continued her work, her knee touching his.

When she was finished, she handed it to him. It was a gift, he realized. Did he want to wear a Hooden crown? He did not, but also did not want to offend Tikidoe, so he wore it until the hunters returned, much later in the day.

*****

Jeek had had a good day on the hunt. He and Gunda had brought down a peccary together, on the way back from the mammoth hunt. As they traveled back, he wore a big grin all of the way. Anything he did with her made him happy.

As they entered the central space together, dragging a skin with the carved-up pieces of meat, he saw Bodd standing with his back to them. Bodd whirled around when he saw them and snatched something off the top of his head. It had looked like the thing that the Hooden leader had worn on his head. Tikidoe stood near him, smiling hugely and showing her large, white teeth.

That was a good thing, Jeek thought. He liked Tikidoe and was happy someone was looking after her.

He received a dark cloud of message from Bodd, though. It was broadcast to all of the returning hunting party.

Why was I left behind? Did no one want me on the hunt?

Jeek understood why he was so angry at being left out. When he had been a member of the tribe, before he fell under the spell of Vala, he had been valuable to the hunters. He was strong and could carve up a mammoth quickly. He had never missed a hunt until he was exiled.

Hama answered the question, her tone as soothing as she could make it, her thought-speak cushioned in a pastel pink, the color of the cloud garments when they were being tinged by Sister Sun as she was preparing to go away for dark time right now.

You were sleeping with heaviness. You have not had an easy time in recent days. It was good to let you sleep. You should go on the next hunt if you are feeling well and after you have been settled here for a bit more.

That seemed to appease Bodd. The scowl left his face and he nodded to everyone, then retreated inside the wipiti, carrying the woven crown.

Tikidoe followed him there.

Jeek and the others continued dragging their bounty into the village as the last brilliant sparks flew from Sister Sun in her joy to reunite with Brother Earth.

*****

Bodd Blow Striker knew that the recent hunts had gone well, but also knew that they needed to do more of them before the Cold Seasons started. Zhoo of Still Waters and her birth sister, Ongu Small One, had finished drying the meat from the previous hunts. Piles of it were stacked inside one of the large wipitis. But all of them knew that more was needed in case sufficient small game could not be caught in the coming moons. They did not know enough about their New Land yet, to be confident of what they would be able to find.

The mammoth herd was still near, still visiting the watering hole every time Sister Sun started to disappear into Brother Earth. Hama designated scouts to make sure of that. Bodd used to be included on these forays before he had been banished. Since his return, he stayed in the village while other males scouted.

It was time now. One more hunt was held. Songs were sung in the dark time before that day, asking Leela, Spirit of the Hunt, and Dakadaga, Spirit of Mother Sky, to grant them success.

The huntresses and the males gathered up their equipment when it was time to set out. Bodd Blow Striker moved to join the others this time, picking up a skin to carry the meat home, but Tikidoe tore the pelt from his hands and grabbed him around the waist, trying to pull him back. Two males usually stayed behind with the Elders and the very young ones.

Hama sent a message to Bodd. *Will you stay behind one more time? This is probably the last hunt of this season. When you have been here longer and are more settled, maybe you and Tikidoe can both accompany the hunt.*

Bodd bowed his head, thinking private thoughts. When he looked back at Hama, he replied to her, *Yes, I will stay behind this time. I am not fully a member of the tribe again yet. I will be for the next hunt, after Cold Season.*

Hama told Fall Cape Maker to stay also, to keep Bodd company, and the hunting party set out in good spirits. If they could bring down two animals that were large enough, this might really be their last hunt for this season. Then they could spend their time curing the skins for clothing and coverings for new dwellings that they would construct when the warm season came again. During Cold Season, they would also prepare the meat and tend to their weapons and tools, repairing them and making new ones if necessary.

Bodd saw how eager, and also how happy Jeek was that he was being allowed, once again, to go on the hunt as a spear thrower. His thoughts radiated. He hoped that this time he might spear a mammoth all by himself. Or maybe with Gunda, which would be all right, too. He walked near Gunda on the way to the place they would hide at the edge of the trees and in the undergrowth until it became the time to throw spears.

*****

Enga Dancing Flower reflected that it had been, indeed, a good hunt. It was over now and all were tired and happy. The males were dragging home the remains of two adult female mammoth and another that was half grown. It had gone better than anyone had hoped for, bringing back three of the huge animals. There would be such a feast tonight.

As they got close, Enga Dancing Flower tried to send a thought to those waiting in the village, to tell them they were coming. But something was wrong. Her thoughts did not reach the minds of anyone. Waves of bad feelings started flowing toward the returning hunting party and they all grew alarmed. Feelings of suffering, anger, confusion flew about with wildness.

Fee Long Thrower sent an urgent thought to her mate, Bahg Swiftfeet. *Run ahead. See what is happening.*

He gave a quick nod and loosened his grip on the skin. The others carrying that skin shifted to make up for his absence and take up the weight evenly. Then Bahg ran ahead through the growing darkness.

What would he find there? There were many questions and much dread. The emanations from the village were so dire that, as they waited for Bahg to report back, all of the recent accumulated terrors ran through their minds as they waited, shuffling slowly ahead a few steps, then stopping. Animals and people lived here that they had not yet encountered. They were sure of that.

The many eyes of Mother Sky looked down on them. They were so calm. But there was not a calm mind in the hunting party.

They were not far from home, so Bahg was able to run there, and to run back, intercepting the group before they reached the village. He withheld his report until he was back with them.

There has been trouble. Tall Ones came and took many things.

Bahg gave them the pictures he had gotten from Bodd and Fall and the Elders. They were depictions of Tall Ones coming from the woods behind their village. While some of the Tall Ones held spears on the Hamapa, who had not had time to grab any weapons, other carried off piles of skins and some of the heavy tusks. He then sent his own image of the empty places where the skins and tusks had been. Several tusks remained, because even the Tall Ones could not carry all of them. But many were now gone.

Hapa sent angry thought-speak from where he was, in the village, to all of them. *Those things were precious. They were our materials to make more dwellings. The Tall Ones have acted cruelly toward us.*

Hama agreed, adding, *This is a disaster. We thought they would be friendly toward us after our first encounter. We were very wrong.*

The returning party made it back to the village as quickly as they could, and then they could see with their own eyes how much material was missing.

Enga ran to the large wipiti and saw that the dried meat was still there. Stopping for a moment to breathe a sigh of relief and collect herself, she sent out a thought with that picture. *I think that we will not starve. We can live as we have been, in the wipitis we have now, after the Cold Season. Then we can get more tusks and skins later. At least, no one was harmed.*

They had had so many successful hunts and had reaped such a large amount of bounty. They had also done a lot of work on those stolen skins. They had been scraped and cleaned, and chewed, to soften them, for long periods of time. Some of them were ready to be cut and made into garments.

Teek Bearclaw was almost jumping up and down, wanting to tell the tribe his idea.

What is it you are thinking, Teek Bearclaw? asked Hama.

We are living among people who are not peaceful, like we are. The Tall Ones are cruel, as you stated. We cannot be friendly with them. There are probably others we cannot be friendly toward. It is time for us to adopt a different way. A way of war and fighting. If we are to survive among these violent people, we must defend ourselves.

The brow of Hama wrinkled on receiving these thoughts. *That is not our way. We are not people who are cruel and violent for no reason. To change our ways, to be like those terrible Tall Ones, would not be a good thing.*

Enga could hear tentative opinions floating around. There were a few who agreed with Teek, that the tribe needed to be more warlike. But most did not think they should.

Hapa thought-spoke to them also. *It is not our nature to be like that. We should not change our nature at this time. We have always been as we are, and we can continue.*

Can we at least think about defending ourselves? Teek asked.

Hapa nodded. *That would be a wise thing to do.*

The discussion was dropped, however, and there was no more discussion of defense. Enga hoped it would be taken up at another time.

For now, though, they had fresh meat and all were ready to cook it for this meal. It should have been a celebration of the hunt, but no one was in good spirits. More hunts would have to be done. Many more.

Enga had a restless night. She had danced as she usually did, but only for a short amount of time and with less enthusiasm than normal for her. She was somewhat cheered by Tikidoe trying to imitate her movements, though. Enga would twirl and Tikidoe would spin, too, all while keeping her eye on Enga, so this made the movements awkward for her. Enga liked to toss her head and swing her long braids. Tikidoe could do those movements, but her curly hair that clung close to her head did not move. She was able to copy the foot movements of Enga very well, though. Having Tikidoe there made the sad night better for Enga.

After the evening was over, when everyone piled into the wipitis to rest, Tikidoe hesitated, looking from Bodd to Enga. Bodd went into one wipiti and Enga into the other, with Tog. The Hooden then followed after Enga and curled up next to her to sleep. Enga was surprised by this, but the Hooden had been with Bodd for all of sun time, when she had returned. Maybe she had missed Enga.

At new sun, Enga made a trip to the stream to get water and Tikidoe went with her. Enga made sure she carried some gourds, two each, so they could both bring water back for everyone. When they got to the edge of the water, Tog Flint Shaper and Teek Bearclaw were there, sitting on the bank, exchanging private thoughts and gesturing toward the water and toward the other bank.

Are you discussing the water crossing you want to build? Enga asked Tog.

He nodded. *Yes. We think we could use a large tree trunk. If we place it from this bank to that one, it would span the river and we could walk across on it. There is such a tree trunk in the woods, not far, that has fallen and is not yet rotted. We could maybe flatten one surface to make it easy to walk on.*

We are trying to figure out how to get it here, Teek thought-spoke. *It is very heavy. More heavy than mammoth tusks.*

It is round, Enga replied. *Can you roll it? You could shape the flat part after you get it here.*

The two males widened their eyes and stared at her.

That is exactly what I am thinking also, Tog thought-spoke. *We could even shape it after it is in place, across the water.*

Teek shook his head, though. *There are many trees in the way. It is not too far into the forest, but there are still trees standing in the way of the path we would have to use.*

Can we cut them down? Tog wondered. *How would we do that?*

Do you remember when Stitcher, the Tall One, lived with us and he made this figure of the Aja Hama that I carry? Enga drew it from her pouch. It was the one she had started putting near the fire when dancing was done so that they danced around it. *Stitcher used a sharp tool to shape this. We would need a very sharp tool such as this to cut the trees. But much larger.*

If anyone knew about fashioning sharp tools, it was Tog. *Yes, a large, sharp tool. We could make that.*

Bodd Blow Striker is also skilled at making both stone and flint tools. He can help, Teek added.

Tikidoe bent down and picked up something. She held it out to Enga. It was the bracelet that Tikihoo, the other Hooden, had worn when she was with them. Enga thought that it must have fallen from her pouch when she got the Aja Hama carved figure out of it.

Enga pictured the ornament on the arm of Tikihoo, who was now dead. The bracelet was made of smooth, polished, shiny stones strung together. Enga had never seen anything like this except on other Hooden females. It would look just as good on the dark-skinned arm of Tikidoe, this second Hooden to live with them, as it had on the first one. Enga took the hand of Tikidoe and slid the bracelet onto her arm, pushing it up high, above the elbow, as Tikihoo had worn it. It was loose, but would be most likely to stay on.

Tikidoe touched it with her other hand, then gave Enga a very big smile.

Enga felt that she had done a good thing, the right thing. She felt Teek trying to send a message to Tikidoe. He cloaked it in dark colors to be private, but he was letting the color slip because the thought was not reaching her and his effort was so strenuous. Enga could read part of it. Teek thought Tikidoe was beautiful.

That is good, was her private thought. *It is good that the tribe accepts Tikidoe.*

The two females made their way back to the village with the water. Enga's thoughts were light and happy. A water crossing would be built. She had made Tikidoe smile. The tribe still had their meat to make it through the Cold Season and they could even get more to make sure they would not go hungry. She raised her face to give a silent thanks to Dakadaga that everything was going so well.

Then ugly thoughts bombarded her and made her stumble, spilling a bit of the water. Tikidoe looked at her with concern.

She does not belong here.

Remember Tikihoo? How we thought she had slain Panan One Eye? Maybe she did slay him. Do we know she did not?

Can we trust this one? She is another like Tikihoo.

Enga almost dropped both of the gourds she carried when all of these hostile thoughts washed over her. A knot of three females were huddled together, throwing out those thoughts. They were not bothering to shield their thinking at all.

Some of the tribal brothers and sisters, Enga realized, were not happy to welcome Tikidoe to their village. Would they try to drive her out? It was good that Tikidoe could not understand the thoughts. That was the one good thing. All the other good things seemed far away now.

Enga tried to make her face pleasant so she would not alarm Tikidoe. But she was so disappointed that the three were Ongu Small One, Fee Long Thrower, and Lakala Running Water.

The two continued on as Enga clenched her teeth so tight that they made grinding noises. She refused to stop and confront her mean sisters in front of Tikidoe. She would let Hama know about what these tribal sisters were thinking, though, and how cruel they were being.

Chapter 7

A team of archaeologists in Spain have really stepped in it this time, but that's a good thing. They've uncovered what is believed to be the oldest fossilized human poo. Five whole piles of it… Geoarchaeologist Ainara Sistiaga identified chemical signatures in the coprolites discovered at El Salt. She wasn't able to identify specific foods, but noted that there's evidence of various berries, nuts, and tubers.

—"Archaeologists have found 50,000-year-old Neanderthal poop," by Lee Mathews, 06.27.2014 http://www.mitbbs.com/article_t/MobileDevelopment/781.html

When Sister Sun rose and met Mother Sky after the dark time, she sent out blazes of color, some the crimson shade of the hair of Enga Dancing Flower, some the golden hue of the hair of little Whim and Sooka. Jeek loved this part of the day even when Sister Sun did not put on a display. He bounded out of the wipiti to greet Mother Sky and to start the day. He was eager to get going because Gunda had said she would go into the woods with him to find soft needles and new leaves for the floors of the wipitis. The flooring had become dry and brittle and needed to be replaced. He also hoped to find some of the fleshy fruit that the other tribe had dug from the ground and cooked in hot water. Gunda had not emerged yet, but Enga Dancing Flower and Tikidoe were coming back from the place in the woods where they all squatted to put their body waste.

The birds were extra joyous today, it seemed to Jeek. Their songs rang through the treetops, greeting the sun with their high noises, chirps and tweets and trills.

Teek Bearclaw barged out of the opening behind Jeek, nearly knocking him over.

Why are you hurrying so, my birth brother? asked Jeek.

His brother stopped and sucked in air while he focused across the central space. His skin grew close to the color of the sunrise today, which was now beginning to fade. Jeek saw that his eyes stayed on Tikidoe.

Do you want to be with Tikidoe? Jeek asked.

That thought is for me, not for you, Teek answered, not looking at him.

That told Jeek what he wanted to know and made him smile to himself. Yes, Teek liked Tikidoe in the way that he, himself, liked Gunda. That was not a bad thing, except that Tikidoe had been clinging to Bodd Blow Striker since she had joined the tribe. Jeek thought a female should prefer his own brother to Bodd, who was a Gata, not even a Hamapa. But he could not tell her that. No one could speak to Tikidoe and she could not share her thoughts with anyone. Unless it would be Enga, soon.

Enga and Tikidoe were now sitting near the fire pit and Enga was pointing at things while she uttered the sounds for them. She pointed to Mother Sky and said, "Dakadaga," the name for the spirit of Mother Sky. Tikidoe pointed upward also and repeated the sounds. "Dakadaga." It sounded more like "Daga daga," but it was close.

Enga then pointed to the dwelling and said, "Wipiti." Tikidoe pointed also and said, "Woopeetoo." Enga had her try it a few more times and she got more close to the correct way to say it.

Jeek hoped that someday Tikidoe would be able to exchange

thoughts, or maybe just words, with his tribe. If that ever happened, it would be because of the efforts of Enga.

Soon everyone was awake and all sat together for something to eat. A large leaf was unwrapped by Hama. It held small nuts that had been picked out of the bristly cones that fell from the tall needled trees. They had been roasted in the fire with the grains the children had collected from the tall grasses. A smell of the roasting fire still clung to them. The leaf also held pieces of the soft, white plant that grew on the trunks of the trees. Another leaf, unwrapped by Hapa, held the plump, sweet berries from the vines that grew at the edge of the forest.

Then Hama surprised them all by presenting to the tribe the fleshy plant they had tasted at the feast with the Yamapa tribe.

Jeek exchanged a private thought with Gunda, who was just arriving. Hama, or someone, had dug up the tubers before he and Gunda could do it. He had wanted to do this first. They could dig up more though, if they could find them.

Yama told me she dug these from the ground and she showed me how to find them, she thought-spoke.

Hapa asked her, *How are they cooked? They are not the same as the ones we had there.*

No, we have no boiling water pit, so I roasted these in the fire, wrapped in leaves. But they taste good, do they not?

The tribe agreed they liked the fleshy ground plants. Enga told them all she was happy to have a new food to eat. *This New Land holds many good things.*

Jeek decided he very much liked the soft, chewy texture and the mild, slightly sweet taste on his tongue.

The day before, Tog Flint Shaper, Teek Bearclaw, and Bodd Blow Striker had gathered a few short tree limbs and split them with flint knives to make flat digging tools.

After eating, those three took the new tools to the banks of the water to dig out a notch in the bank that would be the right size to hold one end of a tree trunk, after they had moved it there.

Jeek almost wanted to go with them, but he wanted more to be with Gunda, so they made their way into the woods, stuffing their waist pouches with fresh, fragrant needles from the trees and leaves from the shrubs as they went deeper into the trees.

I am worried about Tikidoe, Gunda thought-spoke. *I have overheard others thinking bad thoughts toward her.*

Toward her, yes. And about her, because she cannot read our thoughts. I have caught those thoughts also. They are not friendly. Do you know why some of our tribe dislikes her?

For no reason. Gunda frowned and looked angry. *There is no reason. They do not know her. They did not like Tikihoo, so they do not like this Hooden.*

I think that they do not like any Hoodens.

I liked Tikihoo. She did not slay anyone. We thought she did for some time, but she did not. Gunda shook her head, thinking about the cruel, unreasonable attitudes of some of her people. *Although I know there can be reasons to dislike all of one kind of people. I understand if we do not like any Mikino. They are all horrible. Not all Hooden are horrible.*

Jeek agreed. They had encountered the small Mikino people on their long trek to this New Land. Those were vicious and mean small beings. There was good reason to dislike all of them.

Although a small part of his mind wondered if some of the Mikino were good people. Kind people. They had not been around them for a very long period of time.

Look! On that log! Gunda ran through some bushes to get to the delicious, soft growths and broke them off the side of the log. They were good to eat uncooked and cooked, both ways.

Jeek ran after her and broke off some also. They continued wandering through the woods, nibbling on the fungus from the log. Jeek wondered if he should tell Gunda about his birth brother, about how he was attracted to Tikidoe.

He is? She seems to want only Bodd Blow Striker.

Jeek grimaced. He had let that private thought leak out. If only he would not be so careless. He answered her. *Teek does not want anyone to know. He does not even want me to know. I wonder if he knows it, himself. But I saw him being drawn to her. He could not look away.*

I hope there will not be trouble between Teek and Bodd.

Jeek hoped that same thing. There had sometimes been trouble, in the past, he knew, when two males were attracted to the same female. There could be the same kinds of problems when two females were attracted to the same male.

Now, though, Jeek wanted to find some of those new foods, the ones that grew underground, that Hama had served, but there did not seem to be any in this part of the forest, no matter how hard he looked.

They both stopped walking when some waves of excitement came to them. They were strong waves and came from more than one person. Jeek could tell that some were from his brother, Teek. Pictures appeared in the minds of Jeek and Gunda. They were of something that was being dug out of the earth on the riverbank.

They both ran out of the woods, to see for themselves, what was happening.

Chapter 8

When Pangaea broke apart, New Mexico's hot and humid river floodplains filled with dense conifer forests, home to sauropods—longnecked, long-tailed herbivores with voluminous rib cages and pillar-like legs… In 1979, two Albuquerqueans stumbled across several half-buried backbones each about a foot long—during a hike in Ojito. Eventually the find was reported to David Gillette, then a curator of paleontology for the New Mexico Museum of Natural History and Science… Gillette nicknamed the creature "Sam," but officially called the estimated 110-foot-long beast *Seismosaurus hallorum*—the earth-shaking dinosaur. Ironically, seismic tomography technology, which creates 3-D images of the internal structures of solid objects, would later be used to look for more of Sam's bones hidden deep in the ground.

—"The Land of the Giants" in *New Mexico Magazine*, March 2014, by Melissa W. Sais

Almost the whole tribe was there already. Enga saw Jeek and Gunda running from the woods. They were the last to arrive at the riverbank to see the discovery.

Bodd Blow Striker held something long and white aloft. It was a most large bone. The most large bone any of them had ever seen. It was shaped like a bone, but was made of stone instead.

What kind of animal could have had a bone like this? Hama wondered, to everyone.

No kind living now. No kind that we know about, Hapa answered her.

There are many more bones here. Teek Bearclaw pointed to the ground where a few more were exposed. They were all made of stone.

The tribe gathered around the unearthed stone bone, touching it and trying to draw mental pictures of the animal that had died and left it there. The bone was too large to be any part of even a mammoth or mastodon. The bone was the size of a large tusk from a mastodon, an animal they sometimes used to hunt. Those animals, mastodons, had roamed in the Old Land, but were not here in the New Land.

They gazed on the bones while the males dug some more of them out of the ground. Several of them hauled the ancient things, earth still clinging to them, to a flat space nearby and laid them out, trying to fit them together, to see what the skeleton of the huge animal could have looked like.

Hama watched for some time, then gave out a thought to all of them. *Shall we delay building the water crossing for this, to dig up these things now? Or should we build this water crossing first, then inspect these things, these bones made of stone?*

There were thoughts in favor of both of these courses of action. They went back and forth with reasons why one should take place first, then why the other should take place first. Finally, Teek gave his opinion. *Hama, you and Hapa should decide what we will do next.*

That brought universal agreement. Hama and Hapa squatted together in a place apart from the others and conferred privately. After a short time, Hama stood and walked back.

Teek Bearclaw, Tog Flint Shaper, and Bodd Blow Striker will continue work on the water crossing. If they need more help, they shall ask for it. While they are digging, they can unearth any more of the bones that they may find and give them to Sannum Straight Hair and Cabat the Thick, who will try to fit them together. Anyone else who wants to work on that can also do so. We can carry on both projects at the same time. We shall also need to carry out more hunts, after the terrible raid, so the Hamapa will have a lot to do.

Enga was excited about all of this activity. Sannum and Cabat were more aged and would not be able to dig well, so this was a good plan. Being curious about these new things, she also wanted to help them to assemble the bones. A very large animal had lived here in the past. She looked at Tikidoe, who seemed just as fascinated with the bones as the rest of them. And as unfamiliar. The Hooden touched the hard surface of one of them with care and with awe. Then she went to be beside Teek, looking at him with clear adoration in her shining eyes.

Enga wondered if she had switched her affection, or if she would continue to prefer both Bodd and Teek. She saw Cabat give his head a slight shake and turn away from Tikidoe. He must be giving up on her, Enga thought. It was curious that the males all liked her, but some of the females did not.

Fall Cape Maker joined the three other males who were to work on the water crossing. He helped move the dirt with his hands, since there were no more digging boards. He uncovered more bones, and carried them to the flat place where the others lay. Sannum and Cabat moved them around, trying to piece them together, absorbed in their task.

Enga joined the old males and helped lift and move the heavy bones, putting them where Cabat and Sannum directed her to. Tikidoe joined her and helped lift the most large, most heavy ones since she was so very strong. The rest of that sun time passed with almost everyone working on either the water crossing or the bones, and a few back in the village performing the usual tribe tasks of preparing food and continuing to treat the pelts so they could be used as clothing and dwelling skins.

A short time later, a wave of anger washed toward Enga. It was coming from Bodd. She stopped working and looked at him. He was gripping the upper arm of Tikidoe with much firmness. She was pulling away and frowning at him. As Enga was about to go over to them and confront him, he let go of her. Tikidoe went to the side of Teek and worked next to him the rest of that day. Bursts of anger toward her continued to emanate from Bodd, though he did not do anything to express that anger.

When that dark time came, Tikidoe did not sleep with Enga and Tog. Enga watched her follow Teek into the other large wipiti. She was glad that Bodd was in the same dwelling that she and Tog were in. Having Teek and Bodd together would not be good right now. The tribe did not need more conflict.

At the next new sun, Tog told Enga he was going to fashion the tool to cut down the trees that stood in the way of rolling the large log to the riverside. He was excited about doing that, she was happy to see. He had never shaped a piece of flint that large before this. There happened to be a very large piece in his stores that he had intended to split for spear heads and knives. But now, he carefully began shaping it to be an axe head, an angled piece that would chop through the trunks of the trees and help topple them to make way for rolling the fallen log to the riverbank. Enga was glad Tog had this work to do. Everyone was happy when they were being useful to the tribe.

It took only the space of a few suns for Tog to complete a sharp-edged piece. He told Enga how Teek helped him tie it to a sturdy stick with thick sinews. They both bounced it off the ground to test how securely it was fastened. It would not do for the sharp flint axe head to fly off while in use and hurt someone. The flint axe head remained fixed to the shaft while they tested it. So, next, Tog and Teek, as well as Bodd and Fall, went into the woods to clear a path so they could roll out the heavy bridge log. Tikidoe followed Teek with her eyes as he left, but she stayed and worked near Enga.

While Tog had been fashioning the tool, the others had dug up many more bones.

Enga eagerly helped the bone team lay them out and, when they could, fit them together. It seemed that some of the very large bones went together to make legs. But how could that be? Each bone was more tall than a person. Even a Tall One person. It took two of those bones to make a leg, from the way they must fit together. She was glad this animal was not alive now. It could crush their whole village by walking through it and stepping on their structures.

Baby Sooka followed Enga wherever she went, and this included the flat place where the bones were being laid out. Sooka would pick up the lighter ones, the only ones she could lift and she would carry them around, strutting in her toddler way, trying to look very important. Enga took such delight in this child. It was hard to believe that Sooka had not come from her own body. She still mourned the child who had come from her body and who had not lived and she always would. That was beginning to be clear to her. She was therefore two times as glad that Sooka was hers to care for.

Every day more bones were added and fitted together. There were so many bones that looked like they should make up the bones that had been inside the back, that they thought this must be more than one creature. The whole tribe was fascinated with the creature and they all tried to picture what it could have looked like.

Tog worked for all of one sun, cutting the last large tree trunk with his axe. Enga and several others were there at this point, curious about the whole process. When he was part way through, the tree swayed and began to topple. He and the others who were watching, ran to get out of the way as it fell. Now they needed to move the fallen trees to clear the path for the large fallen log.

At last, the way was clear and the path was ready for the whole tribe to help roll the heavy trunk into place, to fit into the notches on either bank. While Tog had been felling the trees, the other males had dug both notches, on either side of the creek.

They would have to fit one side, then make their way to the other side and, standing in the water near the bank, attempt to lift the other side into place. That was the way they had figured out how to do it.

It would be best if a tall tree grew on the bank and could be cut down to lay across the river, but there were only small bushes and very young trees there.

Some of the males had tried lifting the log and most of them were confident they would be able to do it together, to get it into the notches. This would all happen at the next new sun. In the dark time before that, a lot of meat was eaten and dances were kept short so everyone would have energy for the task.

Bodd Blow Striker did not agree, though. At the gathering, he had a public discussion with his brother, Fall Cape Maker. *We should push the log, not roll it,* Bodd thought-spoke to him. *It must be in the proper position when we get it to the bank.*

We cannot move it that far if we do not roll it, Fall insisted. *You are the only one who wants to do it this way. It is not a good way. It is stupid.*

They both stood and faced each other, both of them tense and looking hostile. Enga grew tense also.

Do not call me stupid! Bodd spit on the ground in front of Fall and then glared at him.

Enga thought he wanted Fall to fight with him, to strike him. Working close to them, sorting and moving the bones, she had noticed tension between them over the last few days.

Since he had fallen under the spell of Vala, Bodd had never been the same friendly person he was when he had first joined the tribe.

Now, Fall and Bodd fought about a number of things, like how big to dig the notch, how deep they should go down to get the bones, and even which one was using the better tool for digging—a flat stick or a sharp stick.

Observing that, Enga had wondered if there was another problem between them, one that was making them angry with each other for such silly reasons, arguing over nothing.

Now she looked at them and thought she knew. They both shot side glances at Tikidoe as they confronted each other. They were both showing off for her. It still seemed that all the males wanted Tikidoe to

70

stay with them and many of the females did not. Enga looked at the Elders. They should be approaching those two, talking to them and making peace between them. But they were not doing that. Instead, Hama and Hapa were looking at each other with frowning faces, almost like Bodd and Fall. Were they in disagreement about Tikidoe also?

Enga approached her leaders. *Hama. Hapa. Do you know that some of our females do not want Tikidoe to be here? They are exchanging thoughts about having her out of our tribe.*

They both glared at her. Backing away with slowness, she realized that she was right. They must be in disagreement about that themselves. This was not good.

At last, the rapid thoughts were getting so loud and so bright, the thoughts of everyone, not just Bodd and Fall, that Hama rose from where she was finishing her meat and stood between them.

No more, she told them. *Go and sit apart and do not argue more now. We all need to work together at new sun.*

Fall had one more thought to give to Bodd. *What happened when you were with Vala and you found Doon? Did you both slay him?* That thought blazed bright and angry.

This drew the attention of the whole tribe.

Doon had been a tribe member whose birth mother did not live after he was born. He had not been given the ability to think like other Hamapa and had to be cared for by everyone. He had been small, with a misshapen head. He had given the tribe much trouble with his slow-witted ways, until they realized that Doon was having thoughts of harming others. When he carried this out, he had been banished. No one expected him to live. Was Fall saying that he had lived and Vala and Bodd had slain him?

Enga sucked her breath in with a loud sound. They had met Doon? It had been long ago that Doon had been banished from the tribe, before they started the long trek, and just after his Passage Ceremony when he had passed fifteen summers. Had Doon followed the Hamapa, then joined Bodd and Vala when those two were later banished?

Bodd, too, became still, in his body and in his mind. Then he gave his thoughts, taking care with them. *We did find Doon. He had been following the Hamapa for a long, long time. When we were thrown out, he came to us. Vala Golden Hair quarreled with him almost every day. Until one day she pushed him into some deep water and he died there.*

And you stayed with her after she did that. Fall stated this. It was not a question. Everyone knew that it was not a good thing for Bodd to stay with Vala after she had done something as terrible as that. But she had done other terrible things before that one and he had not left her then, either.

Then the two of them both obeyed the Hama and sat far apart for the storytelling, which was next.

Chapter 9

Mootak Big Heart surprised everyone with his Saga. He told everyone that he had found a new Saga, one they had never heard. It was the Dragon Saga, he told them. The first thought of Enga was to wonder where it had come from. Where had he found it? Had someone else told it to him? And what was a Dragon, Enga wondered? She did not know of such a thing.

He stood, raising his arms and his face to Dakadaga. Enga wondered if he was giving her own personal thanks for the new Saga. Then he sat and started imparting it.

In a time long ago, before any of the Hamapa were born, before any beings of other kinds were born, large animals roamed Brother Earth. He was new and young and was happy to feel their heavy treads on his surface. These large animals were not like any creatures that are living now.

One such animal has been found by us. It has been dead for longer than the memory of anyone alive. The legs of the large animal stretched to be more high than two Hamapa, with one on the shoulders of the other. The length of the beast was more than the distance across a large village.

Enga wondered what he was saying. He was telling them what they had all observed about the animal who had left the bones. Was this a Saga? Sagas were retellings of things that happened in the past. Tales and lore that were from memory, that had been in the memories of ancestors and had been passed down. This did not seem like a Saga.

This large animal was a combination of everything that lives now. All animals came from this one. It was like a fish, like a lizard, like a mammoth, and like a bird. It had wings to fly and the lungs of a fish to breathe beneath the water.

Enga felt growing doubts coming from the rest of them. This was not a Saga anyone had ever heard. Had Panan One Eye imparted this to Mootak? No, she did not think so. This telling made her a bit uneasy.

The large animal could also breathe out fire. That is how fire came to be on Brother Earth.

Now the doubts drowned out the Saga. Hama thought-spoke. *Hava, Storyteller, this is not a Saga.*

Mootak nodded his head to Hava. *This is a New Saga. It is one that came to me. It did not come through Panan One Eye and all of the ancestor Storytellers. It is a new one. It is mine. It is the Dragon Saga.*

There was even more stirring, furrowing of brows, and rapid flinging of thoughts. This was something new. Did they like it? They did not know. Enga decided she did like it. It was exciting to think about a creature, a Dragon, who breathed fire and who flew, even though it was so gigantic. There was no one to say how this creature had lived. This Saga was fun. Even if it had never been true. She knew, though, that some of her tribemates never liked anything new. Even though they had all been forced to deal with so many new things recently.

If a creature had bones made of stone, they would withstand any fire that the creature breathed. The story made sense and was fun to think about, to her.

She looked around for Sooka, as she did at regular intervals. Sooka had been making marks in the dirt with Whim and Mulee, one of the young sisters of Gunda. But now, the little sister was there and Whim was there, but Sooka was not.

Rising and going to the place where the children played, she asked them where Sooka was. Whim was too young for thought-speak, but he gave her a picture of Sooka following someone into the woods. Mulee, the most young sister of Gunda, told Enga that she had not seen Sooka leave. But she knew Sooka had been gone for most of the Saga.

Enga ran to the woods, her heart beating more fast than the drum of Sannum had ever beat. She could not detect the presence of Sooka anywhere. Neither her smell, nor her thoughts. An emptiness rose inside her, making her feel cold, and a little bit sick. She called for Tog to help her search for Sooka.

The Saga was over. Tog relayed the desperate message of Enga to everyone and they began to stir. They rose and began calling for her and searching. When Sooka was not found right away, all of them became worried.

Soon, the whole tribe was searching. They had all been so absorbed in the New Saga that they had not paid attention to anything else.

Fall Cape Maker gave another alarming thought to them all. *Cabat the Thick is also gone.*

Now they all asked each other when he left. No one had seen him since the Saga began.

Calm settled upon Enga. Sooka was with Cabat. They had gone somewhere together. After a very few moments, when no one could reach the mind of Cabat, the calm vanished, leaving Enga more jangled than ever.

She tried to think with calmness. Cabat and Sooka were not at the Saga, not at the end of it. Who else had not been there? She felt that some others had been missing, but could not make her mind clear enough to think who they were. Had she recently seen Teek? Fall? She could not tell.

Enga felt her heart speed up and had trouble drawing her breath in and out. She started shaking until her legs would not hold her and she collapsed onto the ground. But she knew she could not stay there. Tog pulled her up and they conferred together.

We must quiet ourselves, Tog thought-spoke. *We must send our thoughts out to find those of Sooka.*

Yes, that is what we must do.

Enga and Tog stood still while the tribe swirled around them thwacking bushes and searching among the many dark trees in case she had fallen asleep in a hidden place.

This way. Enga could not detect Sooka or Cabat, but she did sense something that was not right. It was in the direction of the place where the trees had been cleared to make the path for the bridge log.

She and Tog ran there, with the tribe following them, as soon as they noticed the two of them leaving.

Brother Moon was showing most of his face and the cleared space was brightly lit by him, together with the many eyes of Mother Sky. As soon as they reached the cleared space, they halted. There was a large lump of clothing, a pile of it, on the ground. Enga recognized the garments on the pile. They were the garments of Cabat the Thick.

She drew near to see that he was wearing the clothing. He lay on the ground, not moving. The Red had flowed from his body. Much, much Red. There was a deep, wide gash in his neck. The tool Tog had made to chop down the trees lay next to him. More Red covered the flint blade. That most sharp flint blade. Enga thought it must be the Red of Cabat. She prodded him lightly with her foot. Cabat did not move.

A thought sprang into the head of Enga, a thought she did not want. She remembered how the tribe had disagreed about whether or not the tribe should accept Tikihoo, the other Hooden, just as they were now doing with Tikidoe. And how they had suspected her of killing Panan One Eye, the Elder who had befriended her. Would they now have a reason to turn on Tikidoe? Even if it was not a good reason. Or even a real reason. Would some say Tikidoe did this? Had Tikidoe been with them for all of the storytelling?

The members of the tribe formed a circle around the body of Cabat. Everyone slowly realized he had been slain. He would never move again.

But, Sooka! Enga's thought went out to all. *Where is Sooka?*

Chapter 10

Jeek stared at the body that had been Cabat the Thick. He had lived a long time, but would never live again. Cabat had been an Elder at one time and had been an important member of the tribe for all of the life of Jeek.

His large body looked deflated now, crumpled on the dirt with a terrible gash in his neck. Gunda stood next to Jeek, staring also, until she nudged him with her elbow. He turned to look at her. She swiveled her eyes around the assembled circle. Then he followed her gaze. All heads were turning toward Bodd Blow Striker. They had both wanted Tikidoe, who was still sobbing for Cabat and standing next to Teek. Jeek thought that Fall Cape Maker might have wanted the Hooden for a mate also.

His thoughts stopped when Hama filled their minds. *We must find Sooka now. Later we will think about what happened to Cabat the Thick. His body will stay here while we look for Sooka.*

She appointed Bodd Blow Striker to stay with the body of Cabat, so that animals did not pull it apart before they could decide what was to be done with it.

Jeek wondered if this was to make Bodd think about the quarrel they had had, and to make him regret it.

Let us see if Sooka fell into the water, Enga Dancing Flower said, before they started their search.

Jeek ran to the edge of the steep bank. The area where the body of

Cabat lay was now trampled and full of the footprints of his tribe, so he could not tell if her small feet had made any prints in the direction of the water, but here, where the tribe had not been, he could clearly see that his were the only footprints in the damp soil here. He looked up and down the bank to see if there were any signs of someone falling down the slope. But nothing had been recently disturbed. If she had fallen into the water, she had not done it anywhere near here. He relayed this finding to Enga, who let him know she was grateful he had checked on that possibility.

He felt they should also try to know who killed Cabat. That person could have Sooka now. Fall Cape Maker? Bodd Blow Striker? Tikidoe?

The tribe was more intent on finding Sooka, though. He put his own thoughts aside for now. Everyone fanned out in different directions, trying to detect the presence of Sooka.

Soon, Jeek detected traces of the jarring presence of someone else. It was not Sooka. He could not tell who it was, but the presence carried an aura of evil intent within it. Was it Vala Golden Hair? Had she been here? Had she taken Sooka back?

Jeek thought that they needed to ask Bodd where the Tall One tribe was, the one that he and Vala had been staying with. But he was not receiving any thoughts from Bodd, even though he was not far away. Was his mind troubled so much with the death of Cabat that it closed off? Maybe he had told someone of the location. Jeek needed to confer with Enga. She had gone in the other direction and was far away, so he sent her a private thought through the woods.

Did Bodd Blow Striker tell you where the tribe of Tall Ones dwells? The tribe where Vala is staying? The tribe he left?

Her answer was swift. *He did not. But it was near the place of the hunt. He appeared there soon after we had slain the mammoths.*

Yes, he had appeared there. Enga was so clever.

Why do you ask me this, Jeek?

Do you detect that Vala has been here? he asked.

The alarm of Enga shot through him. She was frightened.

No, but if she has, then it was she who took Sooka. We must tell Hama. I do not want Vala to have Sooka. We must find her.

They both sent messages to Hama together, telling her that they thought Vala might have been there, outside their village, maybe, waiting to take Sooka. Enga had not detected Vala, but she had been feeling an evil emanation for some time now. It was possible that it came from Vala. If Vala had been lurking here, she had probably disguised the identity of her thoughts. She would not want the Hamapa to be able to detect her.

Maybe Sooka followed Cabat to the edge of the water, Enga thought-spoke. *But who had killed him? And where was Sooka?* Enga knew that someone from her tribe may have done it.

Jeek could feel Hama turning things over in her mind. At last, she sent a thought, private to both of them. *Have either of you detected the presence of Vala since the last hunt? I could sense something, but could not tell what, or who.*

Jeek and Enga told her they both felt exactly that in the same way.

If Vala been lurking outside the village, Jeek wondered, how long had she been doing that? It sent a finger of cold up his back to think about being watched by her. He had another thought. Maybe they were being watched by a hostile tribe. He did not know which of those would be the worse.

After bowing her head in private thought for a moment, Hama sent a thought to the whole tribe. *Let us search this area at new sun and keep searching until there is no more light. We will do this for one sun. Then we will meet to discuss the next step.*

*****

At the following sun time, Sister Sun did not show them her shining face. Instead, Sister Sun drew her thick cloud garments close to her and hid deep inside them. Still the Hamapa tramped through the woods for part of the day, then crossed the stream and searched the flat land there. However, it would not be easy to see anything with the many clumps of pine trees and large shrubs that grew there. Also the pine could mask the scent of a person. The tribe used the branches of the pine to do that when they hunted in this place. Although Enga did not think her tribemates were looking for the scent of Sooka. Scent was usually searched for when they were hunting for food, for large animals to bring down.

Enga grew impatient. She thought they should be tracking with the scent of Sooka. Looking everywhere with their eyes, and reaching for her thoughts, this was the wrong way to bring back her baby. It was not working.

She sent messages to Tog and to Jeek. *Before the scent is gone, I must try to track Sooka. Will you help me?*

They both agreed and soon they left, making sure that no one saw them go. Enga went back to the central place of the village, to the last place she had seen Sooka. She saw an object on the ground, almost trampled into the dirt by the many who had searched this area. She knelt down and pried it up. With a great deal of distress, she sent the picture of it back to Tog.

It was a small carving of a mammoth, done from a piece of mammoth tusk. Tog had made it for Sooka and it was her favorite toy. She carried it everywhere.

Enga was determined to find her. She would follow the scent of Sooka from this place and would find her.

Jeek and Tog trailed after her, but they did not seem to be able to smell the trace of Sooka that Enga did. It was always more easy for Enga to smell the child. But other odors abounded. The vegetation, small animals, the air—damp and heavy, and their own tribe members.

Enga was able to follow the scent of Sooka from where she had played with Whim and Mulee at the edge of the gathering, with Tog and Jeek accompanying her. The trace of Sooka was very faint, and was mixed with the scent of every other tribe member. First, it led to the place where the body of Cabat had been found. So Sooka must have followed him away from the group, as Enga had thought. After that, Enga could follow the trail for a distance, but soon she grew confused.

They were now past the place where the others peered into shrubs and behind and between large trees. They were going in the direction of the hunt, and in the direction of the place Bodd Blow Striker had appeared to them. Soon, they would pass into a stretch of more open land. The breath of Mother Sky blew strong there this day.

Tog put his hand on her shoulder. *Enga Dancing Flower, how are you able to track Sooka out here, where the breath of Mother Sky does not stop, where every scent blows away as soon as it is sent into the air?*

Enga slumped. *I cannot. I cannot detect any trace of her at all. Now it has vanished. But what shall we do? We must find her.*

Jeek had an idea. *If we think that Vala Golden Hair took Sooka, then we should go to the place where the Tall Ones dwell. They might be there.*

There is more than one group of Tall Ones, Tog said. *There is the group that lives deep in the forest behind our village, and there must be another group across the flat land, near to the watering hole where we hunt. Where Bodd Blow Striker found us.*

Let us go there, Enga stated. *That is the only thing we can do.*

The three of them headed in that direction. They soon realized that the night air was laden with even more scents than the daytime air. Some of them were very strong. Mostly they were the scents of larger animals that came out at dark time. Some were scents of fragrant trees and plants. They all mixed together in the air, which was stirred by breezes.

They had not traveled very far, when Hama sent out an urgent summons, calling everyone back to the village. The summons was as bright as thoughts could be, the color of fire. There was danger. They started to run back. Enga cried on the way. She wanted to keep trying to find her baby, but she could not ignore this summoning.

Chapter 11

"The bow and arrow is an ancient weapon—going back at least 71,000 years, a study in *Nature* suggests. Archaeologists working at South Africa's Pinnacle Point cave site uncovered a collection of tiny blades, about an inch big, that resemble arrow points, likely belonging to prehistoric bow and arrows or spear-throwers."

—"Early bow and Arrows Offer Insight Into Origins or Human Intellect," by Erikn Wayman, Smithsonian.com, November 7, 2012

Still frantic about not being able to search for Sooka, Enga reluctantly followed Jeek and Tog back to the village, dragging her feet and falling behind those two, who ran ahead of her and were soon out of sight. All the way back she thought about turning around and searching alone, but that would not be right. Her tribe needed her. But she needed Sooka. The argument went on inside her head as she walked.

She reached the village after Jeek and Tog and came upon a huddle of Hamapa, all gesturing and exchanging thoughts in a jumble. As she drew close, she could see by the firelight that there were other beings in the middle of the huddle. Peering between her tribal brothers and sisters, she was able to see that three Yamapa sat on the ground, surrounded by standing Hamapa. The Yamapa all wrapped their arms around their legs and rocked. Two of them shed water from their eyes.

It glistened on their thin cheeks in the light from the flames. The third raised her face to Hama. It seemed she was answering a question.

Yes, all are gone. All of the rest of our tribe... all gone. All are slain. We only survived.

Hama asked, *Were none of you out of your village? Hunting? Gathering food or other things? Making waste in the woods?*

Enga realized the one Hama spoke to was one of the co-leaders of that tribe, the tribe they had gathered with for a meal so recently. This was either the Yama or the Yama Doe. She could not tell which one was which. She was surprised to see that the clothing of the speaker was dirty and torn, and also the clothing of the other two.

The Yamapa leader answered Hama. The Hamapa all stilled their curious minds to hear what she had to tell them. *We were all gathered for our evening meal. We had just started eating and they came from the woods, making such loud noises that we were all frightened.* She bowed her head and closed her eyes and they could all feel the terror in her thought-speak. *They had many weapons. We could tell that they were there to slay us. They started with those who were close to them, spearing them where they sat. Then our people started running and the Tall Ones ran after them, throwing spears at them, like they were prey, and also using the other most fearsome weapons. Some of us would not run, but stayed to try to protect the children. But they perished and all the children perished. Only we three escaped. We were at the far side of the circle and ran away first.* The Yama, or Yama Doe, stopped to sob. Then continued, gulping for air. *I did not think they would kill all of us. I thought more than we three would be able to get away.*

Hama asked, *What are the fearsome weapons you speak of?*

The Tall Ones can propel shafts with sharp stone tips from a stick with a string that they pull back. The shafts with the sharp tips travel very far and with much speed. She sent them a picture of the shafts and of the bowed wood devices that propelled them. *It was almost impossible to escape from those. They also had fastened the sharp points of antlers to the ends of their spears, which they hurled at some of us.*

Enga shuddered at the mental picture being sent with the words, a picture showing how it was that the Tall Ones could fling sharp stones on shafts from the devices they held. She could see those sticks with the stones fastened to them in her mind as they hurled far and fast through the air to slay the Yamapa, exactly as they were telling her own people.

Hama stooped to touch the shoulder of the crying Yamapa, who gave her a grateful look.

How many suns ago was this? Hapa asked.

The other two looked up and conferred with each other. *A few suns ago. Maybe four. Maybe five.*

Where were you all of this time? Were you hiding from them?

We were afraid to go back in all that time. We got thirsty and hungry and finally had to return. But everyone was dead, even the new babies. The bodies were all still there, some of them piled on top of each other. One pile held the children at the bottom and those who tried to protect them on top.

Enga received the picture of this that was sent out. She squeezed her eyes shut to try to block it from her mind. That did not work.

Did you have no weapons near? Hapa asked.

They were all in one pile and not near enough. They had been placed there, to the side, because we were going to bless them after we ate, for a hunt the next day.

Every Hamapa was stunned by the report. The mind of Enga stopped, frozen, full of the horror. She felt she could not make her thoughts work. Then questions sprang up from her tribe. How could such a thing happen? How could the Tall Ones slay almost an entire village? What reason could anyone have to do something like that? It was like they were a whole tribe of people who were as evil as Vala Golden Hair, or maybe more evil than that, even.

Enga noticed that the three surviving Yamapa had been given gourds of water.

Now, Hama told them, *you must eat.*

It was a solemn meal, and very quiet. There was no singing. No dancing. Not even a Saga. Enga could tell that the Storyteller was a bit upset at that. He must have had one that he was eager to tell. But it would not be right for them to listen to something for pleasure now. Not only was the Yamapa tribe slain, Cabat the Thick lay dead by the river, and Sooka was missing.

Akkal wept as he tended the fire, forcefully throwing twigs in the fire to keep it going. He seemed to hurl the twigs with anger. Before the gathering was over, he went to guard the body of his birth father and Bodd came back to eat.

The visitors had eaten a lot. Enga could tell they were trying to not eat all of the food, but they must have been so hungry. Going without enough food for three days must have been hard. They could maybe have picked the berries that were ripe now, and eaten some other plants, but they would have no meat. It was probable that they did not dare to venture anywhere, even to bushes of berries. They would not dare to hunt because then they might be found if the Tall Ones were still near. Besides, they had no spears, or even knives.

After everyone ate, Hama told the Healer, Zhoo of Still Waters, to take the three visitors to the wipiti of the females so they could lie down in comfort and rest, after a trip to the woods to relieve themselves of waste.

Now, Hama said, *we must make a big decision. We must make it soon. The Tall Ones could attack us next.*

Hapa nodded. *It is dangerous to stay here. We are not far from where the Yamapa were.*

Yes, Hama answered. *We have to move our village. It must be done soon.*

Enga was certain that Hama and Hapa had been thinking together about the subject before this.

It was decided to send out scouts to find a new place. Enga could tell that Tog was sad that the water crossing would not be completed. She was sad also, that the rest of the bones would not be dug up and assembled. At least they had gotten a New Saga from the bones. She hoped the Storyteller would give them more of those New Sagas. The old ones were good and they must hear them so all would learn from the past. But it had given her so much joy to hear the new one, the one that was not real, but came from the inside of the mind of the Storyteller.

At new sun, three males were sent out. Bahg Swiftfeet, Tog Flint Shaper, and Teek Bearclaw. Before the attack by the bear had scarred his back, Teek had been known as Teek Pathfinder. He was still good at tracking and finding.

Enga sulked when she learned that Tog was going to scout for a new location for the village. She wanted him to help her find Sooka. Teek would be a big help also, if she could convince him to do it. Wet ran from her eyes as she thought of Sooka crying for her, being afraid. Was she hungry? Was anyone giving her water, milk? Food? Clean skins to wear? How good that it was not cold now. She would not die from being frozen in this weather. But Enga could not touch the mind of the child no matter how hard she concentrated. That caused her much anguish. When she had gotten Sooka back, and she did not let herself think that this might not happen, she would work diligently with Sooka on her exchanging of thought-speak. Sooka had never been fluent, but Enga would see that she was, after this.

While the scouts were out, the tribe took care of the body of Cabat the Thick. Four Hamapa males were required to lift him onto a mammoth skin and carry him to the flat rock, where they exposed him. He was as heavy in death as he had been in life. Maybe more heavy. Hama rubbed his skin with animal fat and all of them scattered grasses across his hefty body.

Then they returned to take up the planning and the tasks of moving, yet again.

As Enga went about the day, collecting water for drinking, working on some skins, rebraiding her own hair and that of some of the other females, she kept wondering if she should take off on her own to look for Sooka. She wove a leather strip with some river shells strung on it into the hair of Lakala Rippling Water, the mate of Ung Strong Arm. Both females liked the shells in their hair.

When would she be able to leave and seek Sooka? How long would the scouts be gone? They had filled their pouches with meat and grains, enough for a few days. She had tried communicating with Tog, but he had not heeded her. Hama had received messages from Teek, so Enga knew that they were not harmed. But Tog was ignoring her. Maybe he felt that he should be with her, helping to look for their child, and felt bad about being away.

Carrion birds circled above for the rest of the day, preparing to swoop down onto the body of Cabat, helping him to return to Brother Earth.

*****

As Sister Sun sank lower and the creatures in the woods grew quiet, getting ready for dark time, the tribe made preparations for the communal meal. Jeek had had many thoughts of the young female Yamapa called Ranga, who had flirted with him when they had had dinner together. Now she was slain, dead. He was unable to keep his thoughts from picturing her, the person she was, the person she would someday have grown to be. Her life had been too short. Someone would have mated with her, she would have received the seed of that person, would have given birth to babies.

Jeek was keeping part of his mind on Enga Dancing Flower. He was worried about her. Her thoughts were so full of anguish over Sooka that they were spilling out. There was room for nothing else in the mind of Enga this day. He wondered if he should set out with her and search, just Enga and Jeek, together.

What is making your brows draw down, Jeek? Gunda had sat next to him without him noticing her approach.

That was unusual. His thoughts were keeping him from noticing his surroundings. That was not a good thing.

I am worried about Enga.

Because she is worried about Sooka?

88

Jeek nodded.

We all are.

Then why are we not out trying to find her?

Gunda took his hand in hers. *We must first find another location for the village. It is for the—*

The good of the tribe. I know. Jeek pulled his hand away. Everything was for the good of the tribe. But this was not good for Enga. Or for Sooka.

He was startled when Hama jumped to her feet. *They have found it! There is a place for us, for our village. It is not too far. We shall start moving at new sun.*

Hama explained what they had found. There was a place where a village had been. A village of people like them. They could tell by the smells left behind. No one was living there now, but they had left behind a few things. There were some mammoth tusks and a fire pit. The wipitis were gone. There was a small stream nearby. The water flowed down from the big mountain they could always see from where they were. The location was at the foot of it.

Why is no one there? Ongu Small One wanted to know. *Were they all slain, like the Yamapa? Will we be slain if we go there?*

Hama grew silent, in communication with Teek and Tog and Bahg. Then she relayed what they had told her. *This tribe liked to eat stag moose. The stag moose herd moved away very recently and they relocated to be closer to them. Our scouts were able to communicate with one member of the tribe. He was returning with some of his brothers to get several sets of antlers they had left behind. I asked Tog the name of those people, but he did not learn that. The males wanted to get the tusks and leave before dark time. Their new village is not so close.*

The tribe discussed all of this as they ate. Some thought that there might be other reasons the tribe left that village. Maybe the Hamapa would not like to live there either.

Hama conveyed another message to all of them. *We will ask the Yamapa when they awaken at new sun about this tribe. They have lived here a long time. They will know if this is a good location or not.*

Chapter 12

Moose (*Alces alces*), the largest living cervids, are solitary animals that prefer conifer forests... Extinct species of moose include the broad-fronted moose (*Alces latifrons*), and the stag moose (*Cervalces scotti*). The broad-fronted moose was even larger than the largest modern moose that live in Alaska. Stag moose were slightly smaller in stature, and presumably in weight.

—*Ice Age Mammals of North America; A Guide to the Gig, the Hairy, and the Bizarre,* by Ian M. Lange, p. 139–140

At new sun, the three Yamapa emerged from the wipiti they had slept in and joined the tribe for the first meal of the day. They again ate much meat. Enga Dancing Flower knew it was because they had been hungry for too long. When they were asked about the empty village that the scouts had found, they said they knew of it.

Yama Doe, who identified herself to Hama, said the tribe from that village had a language that was a bit different. They were people like the Yamapa and the Hamapa, but they called themselves Ha Kair, People of the Heart. *They wanted to eat nothing but stag moose. We could not share anything with them. They did not want to trade skins or tools, or anything. We did not see them often.*

This was the same information the scouts had gotten from the Ha Kair male who had returned to retrieve the antlers, so they knew it was true.

The Hamapa all agreed they would not try to contact the Ha Kair, wherever they were now. There would be no benefit to the tribe of doing that. But the Hamapa would live in the village they had abandoned. Enga thought her people were lucky they had not been attacked during this last dark time.

Yama and Yama Doe asked if they could remain with the Hamapa and travel to the new place, along with the other survivor, the young male called Waid, since they could not return to their destroyed village. The discussion of this was brief, as all agreed they could stay with the tribe. Where else could they go? Their people were all dead. And everyone liked them.

After they had eaten, Hama had something to tell them. *We welcome you to our tribe and are grateful that you are here. We remember how you stopped the fighting when the males were drinking old juice. I would like to thank you, Yama and Yama Doe.*

Those two approached her when she beckoned them. Hama removed two of her braided hair bracelets, one of bright red hair and one of golden hair. *Yama, accept our thanks.* She handed the reddish one to the twin nearest her. *Yama Doe, please also accept our thanks.* She handed the golden one to the other Yamapa.

Enga and everyone else sent warm thoughts to them. It must be hard to have been a leader, and to lose that position. Would they be happy to be mere members of her tribe? She did not know.

Now I can tell them apart, Enga thought to herself. *Red bracelet is Yama and gold bracelet is Yama Doe.* She wanted to be able to address them by their proper titles. Even if they were no longer leaders, they could still be called Yama and Yama Doe.

After this small ceremony, all began loading extra skins and food onto carrying skins, threading poles in them so that they could be dragged with more ease. The young Yamapa male, Waid, was strong and they were glad he was helping them. Then they started to dismantle the two large lodgings. Shortly after high sun, the three scouts returned and began helping. It soon became apparent, though, that all of the tasks would not be completed in enough time to make the trip during the time Sister Sun was awake. They did not want to be out in the woods, unprotected, during dark time. All kept working so that they could leave at the next first signs of light.

Enga grew more and more impatient. Everything was taking too long. When could she go look for Sooka? Her breathing grew rapid at times and she had to stop what she was doing, stay still, and sit to let her breath slow.

The weather was still fine. There was no indication that Mother Sky would shed tears on them any time soon. She seemed to be smiling on the tribe and their move.

It was a good thing that the tribe would be traveling in the direction from which Bodd Blow Striker had come, the place where Vala Golden Hair was living, he said. If Vala had taken back Sooka, they should both be there. A few times during her sleepless night, Enga had thought she was receiving faint thoughts from Sooka. They were sad thoughts, but not distressed. No one, it seemed, was hurting her. Vala had hurt many people, but Enga did not think she would hurt her own daughter. Still, Enga wanted to retrieve the baby who was now really hers as soon as possible.

They all slept in the open, without their dwellings, and it reminded Enga of the time they had spent on the long trek, coming here. That made it even more difficult to sleep. The trek had not been a good experience. She never liked remembering it.

Before high sun, and after a lot more hard work, they were ready to set out. Hama marked the occasion with an official Pronouncement. She raised her thin arms and rattled her gourds.

"Hoody! Hama vav."

Listen! The Most High Female speaks.

"Hamamapapa poos too. Nasa mana."

93

The Hama leave here. We cannot stay.

"Poos wa tiki vis."

We move near the large hill.

"Dakadaga sheesh Hamamapapa."

The Spirit of Mother Sky, bless the Hamapa.

They left without a song of blessing. There were a few thoughts sent out about that. Some of them let it be known that they would like to do that. They thought it was a mistake not to ask for blessing. The departure seemed abrupt to Enga, too. But it was urgent that they get away before they were attacked by Tall Ones. Some of her brothers and sisters were near panic, broadcasting jagged, rough thoughts.

All of them picked up and carried, or dragged, what they could, and the Hamapa left, along with the three Yamapa, giving long backward glances at the place they had picked, the place they had hoped would be their home for many seasons. Some even had wet leaking from their eyes. They all stopped and stood for a moment, dropping their loads, when they got to the place where they had been building the water crossing, and the flat area nearby where the bones were laid out.

Dragon bones, many of them thought, as they picked up their burdens to continue to another new place.

The ground was still dark with the spilled Red of Cabat. Enga stayed, staring at the spot as the others moved on.

Something was wrong. She closed her eyes to envision seeing the body there with the weapon beside it. Then it came to her. That was it! The weapon was gone, the tool Tog had made to cut down the trees. She alerted Hama and Hapa. They acknowledged her message, and a short time was spent looking for it, but the tool was nowhere to be found. Everyone was puzzled as to what could have happened to it. Were they going to move on without ever solving that mystery, or the mystery of who had slain Cabat? Enga would not let this happen. If not now, later. She would find his killer someday.

Memories surfaced and hung in their minds as they trudged across the expanse of flat, forested land, the trees buzzing with insects, and the rustling undergrowth sheltering small animals that scurried away when they approached.

There were more memories in their minds of the long trek they had made from their home at the edge of the Great Ice. They had watched as that great, white, frozen cliff grew ever more close, each Cold Season. The breath of Mother Sky had grown more and more cold, more and more stiff, more and more dangerous. Even Brother Earth had felt more hard and hostile as time went by. All of the plants had died before the encroaching Great Ice so that an area where nothing grew, a vast tundra, had stretched before the edge of the mighty ice. Many animals had fled. When the mammoth fled, those huge animals that the Hamapa depended on for so much, they had to flee also.

The trek had been long and arduous. Much had gone wrong. Some had died along the way. Enga had carried a child inside her and lost it on that trek. But most of them had made it to the New Land.

They had all vowed never to make such a journey again. This, they told themselves, was not such a journey, on this day. This was a small trek that would only take the length of one sun period.

Before too long, Lakala Rippling Water started a song to keep up the spirits of her tribal brothers and sisters. It was a Song of Thanks for the new place. Enga wanted to dance to the notes. She wanted to hear the drum and the flute, but that was not to be at this time. That would happen in the new place. They must keep walking, keep trudging with their heavy burdens, until they reached the new place. But she could walk with her steps keeping the rhythm of the music.

The new village had only been seen through the minds of the three scouts. But, to Enga, even viewing it like that, it looked like it would be a good place to live. There was the sheltering mountain close by, the large hill that was seen from far away and also from the village they had just left. It would guard them on one side. The new place was in the shadow of that mountain for the first part of every day. There was a stream nearby also. If the mountain held a cave for their rituals on that side, above them, it would be near and that would make this even a better location than the one they were leaving. They had found a cave on another part of the hill, but it was not close to where this village would be.

Tog overheard her thoughts. *I think I saw a cave part way up the hill on this side when I was there.*

How large do you think it is?

Large enough. It looks to be about the same size as our Holy Cave, in the Old Land, the cave we left many moons ago. Maybe a bit smaller.

That thought gave Enga more energy to keep going through the intense heat and the tall grass and the dense prickly shrubs and the many buzzing insects that wanted to fly into her nose and mouth. This place would be better than the one they had picked when they arrived in this land. Everything was going to be better now.

As soon as she found Sooka and brought her back.

Chapter 13

Evidence from bones found at one of the world's most important fossil sites suggests that our hominid predecessors may have dealt with extreme cold hundreds of thousands of years ago by sleeping through the winter… The conclusions are based on excavations in a cave called Sima de los Huesos—the pit of bones— at Atapuerca, near Burgos in northern Spain… These fossils date back more than 400,000 years and were probably from early Neanderthals or their predecessors…the fossils found there show seasonal variations that suggest that bone growth was disrupted for several months of each year.

—*The Guardian*, Robin McKie, Science Editor, 20 December 2020, from a paper published in the journal *L'Anthropologie* by Juan-Luis Arsuaga, December 2020, found at

https://www.theguardian.com/science/2020/dec/20/ early-humans-may-have-survived-the-harsh-winters- by-hibernating

It had not taken the tribe long to set up the new dwellings. They again erected the two large ones they had been using. The work went quickly with the eager help of Yama, Yama Doe, and young Waid.

Then, using all the material they had brought with them, they were able to begin to construct two more that were small. Hama and Hapa would use one and the other would be reserved for coupling, for private meetings, and other things until they established a new cave, a new Holy Cave. After that, they would be able to have birthings in the cave and tend to females having their first Red flow. Neither of those things seemed to be happening soon, but they would someday.

Jeek was glad the move was over and hoped they would never make another one. The tribe had been in the old village, the one where he was born, from where the Great Ice made them move, for many ages.

For the first three suns, everyone worked hard on construction. Mother Sky did not send her tears, so all stayed dry during that time. Her breath was still warm. It was not as hot as it had been for so long, though. Still, they all shed much sweat and drank very large amounts of water while they toiled.

They all worked for the whole time of light, only stopping to eat, a few at a time, with no community meal at dark time. Everyone was so tired by that part of the day.

Jeek tried to touch the mind of Enga several times, but could only detect her heaviness, her worry about Sooka. That, and her impatience with every passing moment that kept her from finding the child.

As Sister Sun sank for the third time in this place, illuminating the rock face above them with a brilliant blaze as She lowered herself, Hama let everyone know that they would have an evening meal of the usual kind. They would gather, have a song, a Saga, and dancing, as well as eating together.

After the meal, where Jeek had been able to sit next to Gunda, Lakala Rippling Water sang a song of thanks for the meal, then the Hava, Mootak, stood to give the first Saga in this new place.

Mootak looked around the circle before he began.

This is the Saga of Cold Season Sleep. Long ago, when our ancestors lived in the most cold places, long before we lived at the edge of the Great Ice, they could not get enough food in the Cold Season. They grew weary and weak. At that time, they all lived in a large cave. When they grew too weary and weak, they would go deep into the cave and sleep for a long time. They would sleep until the warm Season came back, and when they could hunt again and not be hungry. In this way, our people of old were able to live without much food for part of the time. When we learned how to dry the meat, so that we could eat in the Cold Season, we no longer had to sleep for such long times.

Jeek had never heard this Saga. He was glad he did not live in those old times, when the ancestors did not know how to smoke the meat to make jerky. His tribe had always had to live mostly on jerky in the Cold Season, before they made the trek to this more warm place. They would do that here, too.

I am glad we can make jerky and stay awake, he thought-spoke to Gunda.

That is a good thing, she agreed.

And I like very much to eat jerky, even when it is not Cold Season.

She also agreed with that. Jeek smiled at her and she smiled also. Jeek felt something warm and soft flutter and stir inside his chest.

Sannum Straight Hair was ready with his log drum as soon as the Saga ended, and Fall Cape Maker took up the flute, matching his notes to the rhythm.

Jeek was the first to rise for the dance, catching the hand of Gunda and pulling her with him. Her smile made his heart dance inside him even more than his feet danced on the earth that would soon become hard and packed. Others joined in, twirling and even leaping around the fire, which sent its sparks and its signal of warmth and well-being upward, toward the eyes of Mother Sky. It also served as a signal, as it always did: Here there are people. All animals must stay away.

Before long, Gunda pulled Jeek out of the circle of dancers. They were both beginning to tire. She touched his face, then touched other parts of him. Jeek felt so happy he thought he might melt.

He closed his eyes for a few moments. When he opened them, to look at the face of Gunda, he caught a glimpse of something else at the edge of his vision. Someone was leaving the gathering. Curious, he sent a private thought to Gunda.

She was as curious as he was, so they followed with quiet and stealth at a distance, like they were stalking prey. It was Yama. Or maybe Yama Doe. She was sneaking away from the gathering. She was too far away and it was too dark to see what color her bracelet was.

Gunda put her hand on the arm of Jeek. *Do you feel it?*

He sent out his senses and nodded. *Yes, there is another person very near. Do you think Yama is meeting that person?*

She looked around to see if anyone else was missing. *But who could it be? Our whole tribe is at the gathering.*

They had to follow her. This was puzzling.

They stayed well behind her. She did not look around and seemed to be intent on whatever her goal was, wherever it was.

Soon they could clearly smell another person. It was a person like them, but did not give off the same odor as a Hamapa or a Yamapa. It was a person from a different tribe, one they had never met before. Jeek felt a bit of alarm. This was an unknown person.

He was also uneasy because they were outside the circle of light that kept predators away during dark time. Every Hamapa knew not to do this. The Yamapa co-leader did not seem worried about it, though.

The insects of the night gave out loud chirps and, somewhere far away, the prey of a night bird or other animal screamed as it got caught. In the distance, faintly, they could hear the music and the high notes of Lakala giving thanks for knowing how to make mammoth jerky. The many eyes of Mother Sky looked down with serenity and Brother Moon, who was just rising, seemed to approve of everything.

Yama, or Yama Doe, crept around a large boulder that had probably fallen from the heights of the mountain long, long ago. It was partially buried in the ground and had some plant growth on it. When she had disappeared, they approached the rock and carefully made their way around it, not knowing if she would be right there on the other side.

She was not. But not far away, they could see the Yamapa and another person, a male. They tried very hard, but could not intercept any of their communications. They were friendly with each other, he could see that, so the alarm about the stranger that Jeek had felt melted away. He was still nervous about being here, though.

The two stood, dark shadows with faint moonlight falling on their shoulders while they exchanged thoughts. They stood that way for some time, then the male reached for the hand of the Yamapa. They moved more close together. Then they embraced.

It was the meeting of lovers, Jeek and Gunda realized. They looked at each in wonderment. But who was this person? He was not known to them.

The large rock was warm from the day as they leaned against it. They watched for a bit longer, then both thought they should go back to the gathering so they would not be caught spying on the Yamapa when she returned.

I wonder if she will bring this male back with her, Gunda thought-spoke. *Where did he come from?*

I wonder about that also. She is moving toward us. We must get back now.

They made it back without being detected and the Yamapa returned alone.

No one else noticed when she joined them, but Jeek made sure to look at her arm. This was Yama Doe, with the yellow-gold bracelet, who had met with the stranger.

Chapter 14

Jeek and Gunda kept track of Yama Doe the next day, uncertain about whether to confront her or not. Her tribal brother, Waid, seemed to be paying close attention to her also. Jeek was not keeping track of her close enough, though, because Yama Doe disappeared for a while and he did not notice until he saw her walking into the village back from the direction she had taken at dark time the day before.

He decided he had to approach Waid. He might know something about this. Waid was helping cut thick slabs of mammoth meat into thin strips so that it could be smoked to make jerky. When Jeek approached, Waid set the blade down and they walked to the edge of the village.

Jeek started by sending a thought. *Do you know what your tribal sister is doing?*

Waid scuffed the dirt at his feet before he looked at Jeek and answered with sadness on his face and in his thoughts. *You saw me watching her then. I have been trying to become her partner for a long time. Even before the attack and the killings, back in our own village. I thought she was willing when we were there, but now she is withdrawing from me. I do not know why she does this.* His lips quivered as he told this and he blinked back his tears.

Have you followed her when she leaves the village? Do you know where she goes?

Again, Waid hesitated before he answered. *I know she is meeting someone else. I do not know who he is.*

Why are they keeping this a secret? Why not bring him into the village and tell us who he is?

I do not know that.

Do you know who he is, Waid?

He denied that, but Jeek thought he might know, and not want to tell him.

Jeek related the conversation to Gunda when she returned from fetching water.

We need to ask her, Gunda thought-spoke. *This does not seem like a good thing. We should not have secrets.*

I agree. We do not know much about Yama Doe. She has not been with us for very long. We have trusted her, but should we?

Too many bad things have been happening. We need to know everything.

They both approached Waid and he agreed to face Yama Doe with them. But before they could do that, they saw her leaving the village again.

Without stopping to think about what they were doing, they all took off after her. The three of them kept a distance between them and her and masked their thoughts, and she did not seem to know they were there. At least it was not during dark time now, so they did not fear an attack from a night predator.

When she reached the male stranger, they made themselves known, by mutual consent.

Waid thought-spoke to her. *Hello, Yama Doe.*

Yama Doe spun around, her face frozen in alarm. The unknown male frowned at them and grabbed the hand of Yama Doe.

What are you doing? Jeek asked. *Who is this?*

Yama Doe raised her chin and answered. *This is Pakk. He is from a tribe called Mapa.*

Jeek knew that word merely meant "People."

Where is his tribe? Why is he here? Why has he not come into our village?

Yama Doe looked at her friend, Pakk, then he answered them. *My people, the Mapa, have journeyed many, many moons. We need a place for a new village. We had sent scouts long ago to the place where your tribe is now and we had decided to put our village there. But now that we have all arrived, we find that you have taken our location.*

Jeek thought about his. What would his tribe do if this happened to them? They would look for another place. *You can find another place for your village. We are here. The Hamapa tribe is living here now. We also came from far away and journeyed long.*

Pakk looked sad. *I do not think my leaders want to do that. They want to live here.*

Jeek answered him. *Our leaders need to talk to each other.*

Pakk shook his head. He gazed at Yama Doe for a long moment, then walked away.

Jeek, Gunda and Waid watched him go. Why would his leader not want to meet Hama? Jeek was puzzled about so much.

Chapter 15

As Yama Doe trudged back to the edge of the village with Waid following close behind, Jeek and Gunda hung back and threw their private thoughts back and forth. They were mostly questions they could not answer.

The Mapa leader must talk to Hama.

How did Yama Doe meet Pakk?

How long have they been seeing each other?

Where is that tribe now?

They caught up to Yama Doe near the fire pit where she had gone to sit, and asked her all of those questions.

I have tried to get Pakk to talk to the Mapa leader. He will not. He is afraid of his leader.

Is the leader a Hama? Gunda asked. *Or do they have a Hapa, like some tribes?*

It is a Hapa, but he is not called that. The leader is called Mapa Pa.

Jeek shrugged. *I guess that is the Hapa of the Mapa.* He had to suppress the projection of how ridiculous he thought this title was. *Why is your friend afraid of his own leader? How can that be? Does the leader not want to protect the people, to work for the good of the people?*

Yama Doe tilted her head to face Mother Sky, where Sister Sun was starting to approach the horizon. *From everything that Pakk has told me, this does not sound like a good tribe to belong to. The leader thinks that everyone in the tribe is there to serve him.*

That is the opposite of what a leader should do! Gunda was indignant. *Does Pakk want to leave his tribe and join ours?*

Yama Doe shook her head. *He does not dare to do that. He would be killed.*

They kill their own people? Like the Tall Ones do? The mouth of Gunda dropped open at this thought.

Waid added his thought to that. *You know that the Tall Ones killed our tribe. How can you associate with such a people? They are like those vicious Tall Ones.*

We are all in danger, Yama Doe told them. *That tribe wants this village. Pakk says they will attack and take it from us. He is not like the Tall Ones, but some of the Mapa are.*

There is so much fighting in this New Land. Jeek had to pound the earth next to him with his fist in anger. *Maybe we should have stayed in our Old Land and starved to death.*

Do not think that way, Jeek. Gunda grabbed his fist and stroked his clenched hand until he opened his fingers.

Can you answer our other questions? Jeek asked. *Where are they? How long have they been there? And how did you meet Pakk?*

Yama Doe fingered her bracelet and nodded. *I will tell you. I met him when I had climbed up the mountain one day because I wanted to see what there was to see far away. To see what was around us. Pakk was climbing there, too. He goes there to get away from the tribe. There are some who do not treat him well.*

The leader does not treat anyone well, you said, Jeek thought-spoke.

Some are treated well. But there are some others, also, who are not treated well. Yet there are a few who are more like the leader, who mistreat the others. And the leader does not protect Pakk from them. They order him to bring their food and water, to clean their weapons after a hunt, and to sit whenever they sit and wait for their commands. To only stand when they do.

Pakk has a terrible life, Jeek thought-spoke. *Are others treated like this, you say?*

Yes, many others. Only a few give the orders and benefit from the work that Pakk and the others do.

I wonder, Gunda thought-spoke, *if the tribe would follow the leader into a battle. I am sure they could not like him.*

They can fear him, however. How many are in the tribe? Jeek asked.

I do not know, but I think it is about the size of our tribe. A few more than all the fingers and all the toes. And I think they have been camping where they are now for half of a moon cycle. I do not know exactly where. She pointed where Pakk had gone. *Somewhere over there.*

Jeek lay awake when it was time to sleep, wondering if they would be attacked. He watched the flickers from the fire dance on the skin of the wipiti through a gap in the door flap. It all seemed so normal. But more evil was forming and it was not far away. He and Gunda and Yama Doe must talk to Hama and Hapa about this as soon as they woke up. Maybe Waid should come also.

As soon as Sister Sun began to show her face, Jeek was awake and waiting outside the small wipiti of the Hama and Hapa with Gunda and Yama Doe. When Hama moved the door flap aside, they crowded inside, before she could come out.

We must tell you something.

Our tribe may be in danger here.

Another tribe—

Another people—

They are not friendly—

They are—

Stop! Hama commanded them, raising her arm so that her hair bracelets slid up to her elbow. *I cannot follow all of your thoughts at the same time. We are in danger from another tribe? Who are they?*

Jeek nodded to Yama Doe and she told Hama about the Mapa tribe, about how they sent scouts, who found this place, but that the whole tribe were not able to arrive here before the Hamapa.

Where are they now?

Yama Doe gestured in the direction Pakk had come from and had gone back to. *They are very close, I think.*

And you think they are dangerous?

The leader is not good to the people.

Hapa thought-spoke. *I know that this happens. It happened to our own people long ago. More than once. But the people can get a new leader, as ours did. Why do they not do that?*

Yama Doe heaved a large breath in and out. *I do not know. I do not know very much about them. Pakk says the leader has faithful followers. Those who approve of him and oppress the rest of the tribe.*

Hama and Hapa exchanged some private thoughts, then Hama addressed Yama Doe again. *You and Yama and I and Hapa will go talk to their leader. Go and eat something and then we will leave. Do you think that you can find them?*

Yama Doe nodded and told them that she thought she could. She thought she could find Pakk, since they had a connection.

Jeek felt like he would hold his breath all day until his people came back unharmed.

*****

Enga noticed the group around Hama and sensed the tension flowing from all of them. She tried to listen in on their thoughts, but they did not make very much sense. There seemed to be a tribe somewhere and something was a threat to them. Would there ever be an end to threats in this New Land?

Immediately after eating, Hama and Hapa, along with Yama and Yama Doe walked away without telling anyone where they were going and what they were doing. Their faces were pinched and their thoughts were tense, though Enga could not tell what those thoughts were about. Enga touched the mind of Jeek, who had been in the earlier gathering. *Where have the leaders gone? What are they doing?*

Jeek did not approach her, but answered that there might be some trouble. *Everyone should keep spears and knives near to them. The Hama and Hapa are trying to make peace with a people who may not want peace.*

What do they want?

They want this place. They want to live where we are living.

Is there no place for us? Where can we live?

Jeek sent back thoughts of agreeing with her questions, but sent no answers. He had none.

Chapter 16

Enga Dancing Flower realized she was holding her breath after the leaders left with Yama and Yama Doe to talk to the Mapa leader. Was it wise for them to do that? According to Pakk, as Yama Doe had told them, some of that tribe were violent people. Would the Hamapa leaders return? Would they be slain? Would her tribe know about it, if they were?

She tried to concentrate on something, but quit every task as soon as she started it. This was a new worry, to add to the one of Sooka being missing. She picked up a piece of hide to scrape, then put down the scraping stone and got up to fetch water. After spilling part of it on her return trip, she went inside to lie down. Moments later, she got up and went outside. Her instinct was to follow them, maybe while carrying a spear or a knife. If Hama had wanted that, though, she would have told them. So Enga stayed where she was.

Tog Flint Shaper was kneeling, not far from where she was, muttering to himself. He was distracted also, she could tell. He was trying to shape a stone into a new spearhead and it was not going well. She tried not to notice when he split it in half, by accident, and flung it as far as he could. It hit a pine tree trunk with a dull thud.

Anxiety and worry floated through every mind and, even though each person tried to keep those bad thoughts to themselves, none of them succeeded. The fear was too strong.

It felt like it had been half of the sun time, but it was only a short time later that the four returned. Hama and Hapa were running, at a trot. Yama and Yama Doe were not far behind. An atmosphere of danger and alarm ran with them.

Keep your spears and knives with you. Put the small children inside. We must be ready.

*****

Ready for what? wondered Jeek. Nothing happened for a bit and the tribe, with caution and nervousness, continued the day.

Later, after the evening meal, he felt a need for comfort and pulled Gunda to the edge of the village, behind one of the large wipitis where they could not be seen. She smiled as he caressed her face, then her shoulders. At first, she leaned into him, but then she drew away, grew stiff. The music of the dancing, still playing at the fire pit, floated out to them.

He looked closely at Gunda and saw the alarm on her face. It seemed like more than the alarm caused by the earlier caution from Hama.

What is wrong?

She shook her head. *I have been keeping my mind alert to receive whatever I can since the leaders left to speak to the other tribe, and returned, and now I think there is something that moves toward us. I think there are some people who are growing more close. They are sending out thoughts about this place. It must be them.*

Jeek was a little disappointed that her thoughts had not all been on him as they touched, but then he was ashamed for being so centered upon himself. They returned to a place where they could see the tribe and Jeek looked around to try to detect what Gunda had sensed. He saw that his tribal brothers and sisters were, one by one, standing still, listening and sniffing into the night air, some of them silhouetted against the flames. The beat of the drum of Sannum slowed, then stopped. Fall quit playing notes in the middle of a passage.

Hama and Hapa, who had been sitting instead of dancing, jumped to their feet.

Then Jeek finally felt it, too.

There was an odor drifting in on the soft night breath of Mother Sky. It came from the direction the Hamapa had come from on their long, difficult trek, the direction of the Guiding Bear that shone down from Mother Sky. And the direction where they thought the Mapa tribe was located.

He could smell people. They were people like the Hamapa and the Yamapa, but they were not them. There were many, many of them.

Hama sent out her emergency thought. *The Mapa tribe approaches. I do not know what the intentions of those people are. When they get here, we will first try to greet them.*

Hapa added his thoughts. *Yes, we must be prepared to greet them. They did not want to talk to us, but they made no threats. It may be that they mean us no harm. It could be that they decided to talk with us. If so, we shall share a meal. But if they mean us harm, we must be ready for them.*

Jeek wondered if this was the truth. Had the others really not said anything? Had they made threats that Hapa did not want to share with them? There had been no specific reports of what happened at their meeting.

Hama continued. *Gather the children in this wipiti.* She gestured to the one near her. *Hapa and I will join them soon if necessary.*

The tribe had kept their spears in a pile, near the gathering, after the warning of Hama. Now, each adult outside the shelter grabbed one. Tog told them that he wished he had the heavy tree-chopping tool he had made, the one that was missing. They stood around the fire with the spears next to them, some of them holding them in their hands. They ceased all of the music and dancing and remained in silence, straining their ears to hear any noises that came to them from the people who approached.

They tried to touch the approaching minds, since they were people like them, but all they could feel was enmity coming toward them.

All of them felt it, but three of them, Yama and Yama Doe and Waid, started trembling so hard they could not stand. Lakala and Fee went to them and stroked them, for comfort, and to try to distract them from their fears. Yama and Yama Doe gripped some extra spears in their fists, ready to help defend the tribe. Waid held a borrowed knife.

Jeek wondered if they were fearing another attack, similar to the one their own tribe had just gone through. They must be thinking about that, he thought. Everyone was tense, but these three were almost unable to remain upright. The whole tribe sent soothing, calming thoughts to all three of them. Yama Doe stayed a bit more strong and steady, but she looked worried.

Enga placed the Aja Hama figure on the ground for them to circle around. Lakala Rippling Water took her cue and sang a Song of Asking, so that Dakadaga and Aja Hama might keep them safe in their new home, if evil were ever to approach. Fee Long Thrower made it be known that she would only ask Dakadaga, not the Aja Hama. She did not think the small figure could help them. They all held spears as they did these things. It made all the movements awkward and difficult.

The people approaching did not appear to them during that dark time, but the Hamapa all slept with their weapons near to them. Some did not sleep much.

Everything felt so strange to Jeek. In the past, his people would never think of having weapons ready when they were about to receive visitors. But now that they knew there were some people nearby who would hurt others, they had to do this. That had never happened in the Old Land. It threw him off balance. Brother Earth felt unsteady beneath his feet.

Jeek also wondered if his tribe would actually use weapons on people. They had never done that. But, in this new place, there were others who did. The Tall Ones here had done that to the Yamapa. He still felt some of the shock he had felt when he learned that it had happened. The Tall Ones they had known before had not slain people, except for one of them, the one who had lived with them. They had all agreed there was something very wrong with that Tall One, as sometimes happened, and he had been cast out after joining them for a time.

Jeek knew that the good of the tribe was what must always be thought of. No actions should ever go against the good of the tribe. They must all defend each other. If the tribe was attacked by people who wished them harm, then they would have to do what they had never done before. They would have to fight them. Maybe they would have to slay them. As a group. Tribe against tribe.

That concept was so different for him, it was hard for Jeek to think it. He wished he had not had to think about it.

*****

Enga felt Tog stirring during dark time.

Where are you going? She sent her thoughts cloaked in her dark blue private color so she would not disturb anyone else.

Someone is outside the door.

She crept to the door with him and found two people there, crouching and looking afraid. She recognized one of them.

You are Pakk, the person Yama Doe has been meeting.

He nodded. *Yes. And this is my birth sister, Deeta. We wish to warn you. And to leave our tribe. To stay here. They will attack you at first light. You must all be ready. Our leaders are cruel people and will try to kill you all to gain this place.*

Why would someone kill people just for a place? Enga wondered. *There are plenty of places to live. Our leaders tried to talk to them.*

I know. But they are not going to do what anyone else wants them to do. They killed the good leaders, the kind leaders that our tribe used to have. These leaders are three birth brothers, and some others who follow them.

Tog and Enga thanked them and took them inside so they could hide there. Then Enga sent out muffled messages to everyone, telling them when they were going to be attacked.

At first sun, the Hamapa prepared for something they had never done before, defending themselves against an aggressor. There had been much discussion at dark time about how to do this.

Hapa had thought-spoken, *The children must be protected. Let us put them into this wipiti.* He gestured toward the large one which was the most near to him. *We should have adults with them. Hama and I will be there. Mootak Storyteller and Akkal Firetender.*

That made sense to Enga. She added her thought. *Pakk and Deeta should be with them.*

Hama agreed. *Yes, let them go there now. The females will be able to throw spears, as if this were a hunt. The males can be behind them with extra spears, also as it is done on a hunt. If some of us are injured, some males can pull them back and tend to them.*

They were ready now with the children once again inside one of the large wipitis with the leaders, and Pakk and Deeta were with them, by order of the Hama. Enga was happy about that. She did not want them to have to fight their own tribe, even if they would want to.

Chapter 17

Sister Sun had just begun to peek over the edge of Brother Earth, rising behind the large mountain, shedding slanting rays across the plains, when a terrible screaming was heard. The Hamapa, who were sitting, ready, jumped up, weapons in their hands, as the village was overrun by a fierce people, the Mapa tribe, the tribe of Pakk and Deeta.

Enga saw, at a glance, that they were the same type of people as the Hamapa. They even wore skins of mammoth hide and carried spears very similar to those of the Hamapa. But there were terrible differences. They had black markings of mud on their faces. These markings made them look fierce, with large eyebrows and lines of anger around their mouths. The screaming would be terrifying in any place, at any time, but was even more so coming from those painted mouths.

One of the intruders ran past the line of defense and drove a spear into the arm of Sannum Straight Hair. Ung Strong Arm immediately threw her spear at that intruder and felled him, her missile piercing his throat. Enga felt her birth sister shudder, and shrink on her insides.

She and her sister touched their thoughts together for a very brief moment, feeling the impact of slaying a human, a person like themselves.

This is not an animal, not something we will eat, thought-spoke Ung, with anguish in her thoughts. Enga gave her what brief comfort she could, knowing that she might have to do the same thing very soon.

Enga, her spear in her hand and slightly crouched to be ready, made note of the fact that all the warriors were males. Where were the females of this tribe? Were they waiting to do battle when the males tired?

She waded into the fray, slicing and stabbing her way through them. She didn't kill any, but injured many. Each time her spear tip pierced the skin of one of them, she drew back in her mind. But she knew she must continue doing this. Must continue fighting to save her tribe.

For now, the battle was fought at the edge of the village, at the place where the Hamapa had been able to drive the invaders. They knew they had to keep them away from the small children, who were all together with Hama and Hapa and the two from the Mapa tribe, in the large dwelling farthest from where they fought.

Little by little, as Sister Sun continued to journey, to rise, then to begin to sink, the Hamapa drove them away. Two more of the intruders were slain by Fee Long Thrower. They lay where they fell. The invaders were too busy fighting to drag their bodies with them. Sannum stayed behind with his arm so injured that he could not wield his spear. He had handed the weapon to one of the females, who gave it to Fee after she threw her first one and hit her mark.

The terrible fighting went on for such a long time that the tribe developed a rhythm. Several females stood in front, piercing and spearing when they could. When they tired, new females came to the front and the recent fighters fell back behind them to gather strength. The males were behind the females, picking up spears thrown by the enemy and handing them to the fighting females. Yama and Yama Doe fought as hard as anyone and Waid helped the rest of the males, supporting the fighters.

Step by step, the invaders, who were all male, were driven back. The Hamapa had to step over the bodies of those they had felled, cringing as they did this. No females from that tribe ever appeared. After Sister Sun rose high, then began her descent, the fighting continued without ceasing. Some of the Hamapa males brought water to give to the females who were not in the front at that moment.

*****

120

Jeek took his place with the females, proud, at first, that he knew how to throw a spear. After Fee brought down her second male, he felt something in his stomach turning over and making him stagger. His thoughts were much like those of Ung, earlier. It was one thing to kill for food, to kill an animal. But now he and his tribe were killing people. He was in the front line when he started to feel sick. He bent over, trying not to throw up. One of the enemy rushed toward him, spear pointed at his head.

Jeek straightened up and raised his spear, catching the male in his neck. The amount of Red that spurted from his neck, splashing onto him, made Jeek feel even more sick. The male stumbled forward two steps, then fell to his knees, then pitched forward, breaking the shaft of the spear and driving the point in more deep.

Ung Strong Arm laid her hand on the shoulder of Jeek. *Go. Go to where the males are. You cannot fight anymore.*

He knew that was true. Even if he had a new spear, he would not be able to throw it, or even pierce someone with a knife. All he wanted to do right now was crawl into a wipiti and lie down.

The fighting continued and the melee kept moving away from the village. Jeek stayed behind, following them for some time, then trudged back to the village. He found Sannum Straight Hair sitting by himself, holding his hand over the place where the spear had pierced his skin so much earlier. His Red was flowing from the wound, so much that a puddle of it lay beside him. Jeek had some of the skills and knowledge of his birth mother, Zhoo of Still Waters, the Healer, from having watched her work for all of his life. After he ran to where his mother kept her supplies, he came back with strips of hide, long wisps of grass, a deerskin bag, and a gourd full of honey.

As he had seen his mother do, he tied a leather strip around the arm of Sannum, above the wound, to stop the flow of Red. He wadded up the grasses to make a small ball that he pressed into the opening of the wound. He then dipped his fingers into the bag, scooped out some bear fat, and spread that over the grass ball to hold it in place. Next, he smeared honey from the gourd on top of everything. By that time, the Red flow had quit, so he slowly untied the strip.

Sannum gave him a grateful look and a weak smile. *Maybe you will be the Healer someday.*

Jeek knew that his older brother, Teek, would be the Healer, but he was proud that he had been able to treat the wound of Sannum. Some of the unrest inside his stomach had calmed down. He sat with Sannum until his own tribe began to return.

They plodded, their steps slow and heavy, through the darkness, into the circle of light from a small fire that Akkal had kept tended. He had stayed behind and had not fought, since he would always be needed for the fire. Neither had Mootak, the Storyteller, fought. They had both sheltered with the children and Elders.

The fighters were all tired in their bodies and in their minds. No thoughts tumbled out. Jeek wondered if they were trying not to think, like he was, or if they were unable to think at this time. He was so tired he didn't ever want to stand up again, so they must all be more tired than that, since they had kept fighting long after he had left the battle. He searched their faces and their minds. All were blank. Some of them sliced off hunks of meat from the stores Akkal had set out and ate a few bites. Some went to lie down until next sun. They had to walk around the bodies of the Mapa that lay at the edge of the central place.

Zhoo, the Healer, came over to Sannum and Jeek and looked at what Jeek had done. She approved of the treatment, which made Jeek feel somewhat better about everything. She left to clean off and put away her weapon.

Hama and Hapa and the others began to come out to greet and comfort the warriors.

Then Jeek sensed that not all of his tribe was present. Someone was missing. Ongu Small One, the mate of Sannum Straight Hair, was not there. Ongu and Sannum were the birth parents of Mootak, the Storyteller, as well as two other young boys. Ongu was also the birth sister of his own mother, Zhoo. Mootak came up to Sannum when he emerged and gave him a private thought. The wet flowed from both of their eyes and they gripped each other tightly, rocking back and forth.

Jeek looked for his mother again, but she was already walking toward him. She pulled him to his feet with gentleness and told him what he already knew, but had not wanted to acknowledge.

Ongu Small One was slain by one of the others. We will go out and get her at first sun. And we will move these slain enemies away also, if their tribe does not come for them. Hama has told us she will decide what to do with these bodies after this dark time, if she needs to.

Two of the males were pulling the dead enemy bodies away from the central place for now. They dragged them into the darkness and left them there. Where they now lay, they would not be protected from night scavengers by the ring of firelight. Jeek clamped his mind down to not follow that thought any further.

Hama told them that she and Hapa would stay awake to make sure none of the invaders came back. The rest of the tribe were to go to sleep.

Jeek thought he might not be able to sleep because his mind was still so troubled by what he had done, but his body was also weary enough that he could not stay awake after he put his head down. He kept a spear next to him, as did many others.

Chapter 18

The next day, Jeek was so weary he had trouble sitting up after his restless sleep, haunted by the vision of the person he had slain. He was not the only one. No one had much energy.

Hama and Hapa went inside to rest after staying up all during dark time on alert, in case some of the Mapa males would have returned to do them more harm. Some of the tribe ate when they got up, some did some tasks, many sat on the ground, staring, with the battle replaying in their minds, over and over. Hama and Hapa remained inside, resting, now that the others were awake.

The males were tired, as well as the females, but they brought food and water to those who had actively fought and were so weak and exhausted they could barely stand. The newcomers, Pakk and Deeta, helped with this, as well as the children. Jeek checked on the wound of Sannum and some of the scrapes and injuries that others had received from the enemy spears.

Finally, when Sister Sun had reached her most high point, Hama emerged through the door flap and stood before them.

We have many decisions to make. Her message was bright yellow-orange and public, for all.

The ones sitting in a stupor roused themselves. Those resting inside came out. All paid attention.

We must first retrieve the body of Ongu Small One, our sister who was slain. This will be the first dead body of our own tribe in this new place. Has anyone seen a suitable rock?

Bahg Swiftfeet showed them a thought-picture of a large flat rock that lay at the foot of the mountain. It was not very near where they were now, but not very far. It was part of the way around the big hill. That was a good location for that. They did not want it to be near.

We will use that rock, Hama thought-spoke. *We will retrieve Ongu Small One from where she was slain and bring her there.*

Sannum wanted to help carry Ongu, because she was his mate, but he could not lift anything with his arm being as injured as it was. Bahg and Tog trotted off to get her, taking some skins to wrap her in. Jeek went with Sannum and the rest of the tribe to the place of the flat rock that Bahg had showed them and waited for their brothers to get there.

To get to that rock, they had to pass the place where the bodies of the invaders had been left in the dark. Night creatures had devoured parts of them, but there was enough left to tell that they had been people. The Hamapa averted their faces and tried to hold their breath from the stench. Insects buzzed above the decaying forms and they had to swat some of them away from their faces as they passed. Jeek pictured the night creatures that had gnawed on them, pulling limbs from some of the dead. He could not suppress the shuddering as he moved past them.

Pakk and Deeta halted and gazed upon the bodies, their minds closed to all others. Jeek could only guess at what they were thinking and feeling. These dead bodies had been their oppressors, the ones who had tormented them. But they were also those they had spent their entire lives with. How horrible it must be for them to be seeing all of this.

The Hamapa waited, a distance away, for those two to finish standing and viewing their tribe, then Pakk and Deeta followed the tribe as they continued to the flat rock.

After Bahg and Tog arrived, carrying the wrapped body, they placed her on the flat rock and unwrapped her. Then Hama smeared fat on her small form, batting away the flies that hovered. In the old place, flower petals or pretty leaves had usually been scattered onto the body by the young children at this time, but in this place, all they had been able to find were plain green or brown tree leaves and grasses, some of them heavy with grain. They threw the leaves, the grasses, and the grains onto the fat-smeared body, then left, so that the insects, the other animals, and Brother Earth could all work together to reclaim her as quickly as possible. Brother Earth and Gongor, the Spirit of Death, would now take over.

The evening meal was solemn. Once again, there was no Saga, nor singing, nor any dancing. Jeek sent a message to Pakk and Deeta that the evenings were not usually like this. They would be more lively at another time. He noticed that they both stayed close to Yama Doe.

Jeek recalled that Hama had said there were many decisions to make. He wondered what the other decisions were. He fell asleep half thinking about that, and still half sickened by having slain a person. But also sickened by everyone who was slain. Would more tribes come to try to overtake this place?

*****

At new sun, some of the gloom had lifted from the minds of the tribe. Fee Long Thrower told Enga that she had been wrong. She admitted that the small carved figure of the Aja Hama had protected them in the battle. Learning this made the heart of Enga a bit lighter. Maybe the whole tribe would someday revere the figure as she did.

Hama rallied them to discuss what to do about the remains of the dead bodies left behind by the invaders.

If they were going to come for them, they should have done that already, she thought-spoke to everyone. She consulted Pakk and Deeta, but they had no thoughts about what to do with them. They told her that they had officially left that tribe and wanted nothing to do with even the deceased members of it.

Enga Dancing Flower wondered what kind of people would leave their own slain brothers behind. How could anyone fault the two Mapa newcomers for wanting nothing to do with them? She could tell that others were thinking the same thoughts. That tribe may look like the Hamapa and others like them, but they did not act like them. Not in any way.

She saw the effect of these thoughts on Pakk and Deeta and amended her thinking to apply only to the rulers, the leaders. There were other people in the tribe who were oppressed and were not vicious, like these two, she knew.

Where did this tribe come from? Where are they dwelling now? Zhoo of Still Waters asked. Getting no response, she directed a thought to Yama Doe. *Do you know these things? Do your companions?*

Yama Doe closed her eyes. Enga thought she must be casting her thoughts to the defectors, Pakk and Deeta, privately.

At last, she sent a thought. *Not everyone has learned about all of this yet. We do know they are called Mapa, the People. They have not been here more than a moon cycle. They have been on a trek, much like you were, and from the same direction. They were also at the edge of a Great Ice, as you were, and were coming to this place. We have a sister tribe, one that we have traded with, that was along their way. They, in turn, had gotten information from another tribe farther away that these were not good people. That they stole food and even children. They slew many people on their way. At first, we thought that they were the ones who invaded our Yamapa village, when our own tribe was attacked. They were not. But I think this must be those travelers we were warned about. They have finally arrived here and want this place for their new village. I know much of this from Pakk.* She nodded in his direction.

Pakk added to these thoughts. *Our tribe did much harm on the way here. The leaders told all of us to steal food and other things from anyone we met. They even killed the ones who resisted and tried to keep their things. It made no difference to them, if the people were babies or children or adults.* The body of Pakk trembled for a moment after this telling.

The information from Yama Doe and Pakk was shocking. The Hamapa had not even received any of these reports that the Yamapa had gotten. But maybe that was because they had not had an established place when this other tribe was migrating and had not ever yet traded with anyone from anywhere near here. They were both migrating at the same time, the Hamapa and the Mapa. Before they arrived, the Hamapa had not met any of those they were now living with.

It almost made sense, Enga thought to herself, that these people would not come back for their own dead. The customs of these were not the customs of the Hamapa.

One more thing that I know about them, Yama Doe added. *They have a male for a leader and all of the hunters are male. The females do not hunt.*

Mind murmurs flew now. How strange these people must be!

We shall need to dispose of these bodies, Hama continued. *This is a thing we have not done before, dispose of bodies that are not ours. Does anyone have ideas on where to put them? How to give them back to Brother Earth?*

Again, Pakk was asked, and he raised his shoulders, looked to Mother Sky and shook his head. He did not want to express any thoughts about this.

It was generally thought that they should not be placed on the rock that the Hamapa had just used, and would use again when one of their members died and needed to be returned to Brother Earth. But the dead could not stay where they were. They would eventually be consumed, but that would take time and would draw more and more dangerous animals close to their village. Already, many insects crawled on them and flew in and out of their noses and mouths. The buzzing could be heard from where they now sat, at a distance from them. The rank odor of death would get worse and worse. Something must be done soon, quickly. But what?

It was Ung Strong Arm who came up with an answer. *Look. See what surrounds us.* She stood and swept her arms toward the woods and shrubs that stretched between the stream by their old village, and this new one. *They can be dragged away and placed on the ground in that direction, far from here, in the undergrowth or the thick trees.*

Her idea met with the approval of everyone. They did not wait. The males jumped up and, taking the corpses by their feet, started dragging them away, into the thick bushes beneath the towering pine trees. They each took several. They went far and were gone for several hand lengths of the journey of Sister Sun through Mother Sky. Sister Sun was kissing Brother Earth when they returned, thirsty and hungry.

Even before they got back, Enga could see the large birds that ate flesh circling the spot where her brothers must have left the bodies. She was glad they could not see the same birds hovering over Ongu Small One, since the mountain was in the way. She did not like seeing those huge birds. No one did.

She fell asleep knowing that she must resume her search for Sooka the next day. If some of her tribe could help her, then that would be good. If they could not, she would do it anyway. Alone, if she had to.

Chapter 19

Enga was awake before first sun. As she opened her eyes, she wondered if she had actually slept, or if she had lain with her eyes closed and her mind running through her fears all during dark time. She was so tired. If she did not have her mission to do now, she could have kept sleeping for a long time.

But the mission was urgent. She pushed herself up, grabbed something to eat, and tried to lightly touch the minds of Ung Strong Arm and Jeek. They were both asleep and sleeping very hard. She could not get through to them. She could have awakened Tog Flint Shaper, next to her, but she did not know if he would try to stop her or not. Tikidoe was not where she could see her. She must have awakened before now and gone out somewhere.

It would take her brothers and sisters a few suns to recover from the battle. Enga's quest for Sooka gave her spirit much extra energy, even though her body remained sore and tired. The sense of urgency grew inside Enga with each moment. She had to leave now. This moment.

Packing some provisions in a large pouch, in case Sooka was hungry, she slung it over her shoulder and slunk from the wipiti, making almost no noise. Straightening, outside the door flap, she saw that the village was still. No one stirred. The first bird of the morning was just beginning its tentative song, warming up before it would soon go full throat and full volume, and the rest of the birds would join in.

It was an effort to draw back from the anger she felt toward the cheerful birds and the beautiful blue of Mother Sky. They all seemed so happy. So serene. Enga was not happy. Not serene. She was frantic.

She probably did not need to, but she hunched down and crept outside the boundaries of the small place, holding even her innermost thoughts in check. She felt that she might be stopped by Hama if she was detected. Not wanting to be deterred, and determined to carry on the search, she let no one know what she was doing. She had no spear, but she did have the knife she always carried in her pouch.

Once she was a good distance from the village, she started casting her thoughts out to Sooka. She turned in a circle, casting sharp, desperate messages, in her own private colors, using soft greens and blues, directing her thoughts only to Sooka. Distance should not make a difference in how her thoughts travelled with her own adult tribe members, but it might be that the mind of Sooka was unable to receive thoughts right now for some reason. The child might be unconscious, or troubled by emotions so strong that they formed a barrier, or…worse. Enga did not want to contemplate what could be worse. She would keep going and hope to get to a place that was near to Sooka so that it might be more easy to break through to her. She only knew one direction to take, so she took that, toward where she thought the Tall Ones were.

The day grew more warm, even though the last few days had been slightly more cool. They were not cool compared to the place where she had grown up, but in this place, the breath of Mother Sky was showing them that it would not be fiery hot for too much longer. As she hoped this day would be more cool, the sweat began to form on her body and to drip off her face.

After several hand spans worth of the travel by Sister Sun through Mother Sky, as she trudged around the mountain toward the place they had encountered Bodd, she grew aware of the thought-tendrils in her mind that were coming from her tribe, reaching through the weak barrier she had thrown up as a thought shield from them. They were from Tog, Ung, and Jeek. Also from Hama and a few others. The stray thoughts told her that they were alarmed that she was missing. For them to worry so much was not something she wanted. Trying to settle their fears, she broadcast back to them that she was searching for Sooka and was not harmed.

Now the requests, even demands, that she return flooded to her. She sent back a terse message. *I will not stop looking until I find Sooka. If anyone wants to help me, I will tell you where I am.*

When no offers of help came to her, she closed her mind firmly. She stomped on in anger at her tribe, her fear for Sooka growing with each step.

By high sun, she had to stop and drink water from the skin pouch she carried. She realized that the rays of Sister Sun were still fierce and that She would never be as friendly in this place as She had usually been in the old village. Sometimes it felt as if She was dangerous, as if She wanted to do harm to Enga and her tribe. Now the sweat poured off the face of Enga, dripping and making dark splotches on her thick, heavy mammoth skin garment.

She had to keep it on, since some of the bushes she waded through had sharp barbs and cut her legs and arms. Most of the insects left her alone, hopping and flying before her as she disturbed them, but some very small ones swarmed onto her face, and some landed on her skin and stung. She had brought a small rabbit skin cape so she could get warm if she were still out during dark time. It was too hot to wear it now, but she had to sling it over her shoulders for some extra protection against the bites and stings. She also unbraided her hair, shook it out, and hung it partially in her face to try to keep the insects away. They droned and whined and whirred as they hopped and flew in the bushes, in the grasses, and in the trees, which grew thickly in some places and were sparse in others.

It was well past high sun when she reached the place where they had met Bodd. Her steps had grown more and more slow and she was not getting very far very fast. The watering hole where they hunted mammoth was just ahead. She plodded forward until she came to the edge of it. Kneeling, she threw off the cape, cupped her hands, and splashed the water onto her hot, steaming face, then threw some more over her body to cool it off. It seemed like the insects had entered her mind and all she could hear were buzzing and swishing noises. Eventually, she realized that the sounds were not from the swarming insects, but were coming from inside her head. She was also so overheated that she was off balance.

There were a few small trees near the water and she stumbled over and rested in the shade of those for some time. There were not as many bugs here as there were deep in the trees. The buzzing noises in her head stopped at last and she felt more cool and calm. She cast her thoughts to Sooka again, then opened her mind for replies. She did not get anything from Sooka, but she found faint thoughts from others nearby. Were they the Tall Ones that Bodd Blow Striker had stayed with? Had she found them? If she had, then Vala Golden Hair should be there. And if Vala had taken Sooka, she would be there also. Her breathing grew more rapid with her excitement about being close to Sooka at last.

Another thought stream came to her, strong and insistent. She turned her attention to it. The thoughts were from Ung Strong Arm. *I am coming to help you. No others can help because of a big decision that was made after you left. I will tell you about it when I reach you.*

Enga let out a short laugh of relief and joy. She was getting help! She relayed to Ung where she was and decided to wait for her before going onward. She had no idea how she was going to approach the tribe, or Vala, and was relieved that she would be able to rely on Ung to help her with that.

Ung Strong Arm was shaking her shoulder. Enga had fallen asleep under the small trees.

Wake up. I need to tell you of the council we had this morning.

Enga scrambled to her feet and embraced her birth sister. *I am so happy you came to help me. I don't know what to do. I don't know how to get Sooka.*

Ung hugged her back, then squatted down and motioned Enga to do the same. *First, let me tell you the news. We met and decided that we cannot stay in the place where we are. Hama sent scouts again to find another new place. They are heading in this general direction, but are not coming right here. The Yamapa told us about a village near here that has been empty for many, many summers. A tribe of Tall Ones lived there, and they joined another tribe and made a large village that is not very far away. They are not violent Tall Ones, Yama Doe told us. They are peaceful and friendly and the Yamapa have even traded with them.*

Was that the tribe that Vala and Bodd had been with? She asked Ung about that. *The tribe that may be very near right now?*

I do not know. It is possible.

Where is it? Can we go there now?

Ung did not know where they were. *But Bodd Blow Striker should know.*

I will ask him right now. Enga sent a message to him and found that he was one of the scouts sent to the location Yama Doe had told them about.

Enga was surprised to get a dark-colored private message from Bodd. *I must shield my thought so that Vala Golden Hair does not intercept it. She meant to harm me when I was there. If she finds out where I am, and that I am near, I think she might try to come and find me.* There was fear wrapped with his thoughts.

After Enga agreed to keep their communication secret, he drew her a thought-picture of the location of the tribe he had sheltered with. Enga shared it with Ung after she finished her private exchange with Bodd. It was not a far distance from where they were now. She had been right about being close to it.

She and Ung had a few bites of the jerky Enga had brought, but she found she could not eat more than two bites right now. Her stomach would roil if she did. Ung had more, though. Then they packed their things and picked up their bags.

Feeling refreshed from her rest and energized to have Ung helping her, Enga set off trotting toward the location Bodd had given them. They should be able to reach it before dark time.

Chapter 20

An ancient femur found in a Chinese cave is unlike any bone formerly discovered, suggesting it belonged to a previously unknown human species that lived alongside modern man just 14,000 years ago. The 14,000-year-old bone fragment, which was found in the Muladong Cave in southwestern China in 1989 but was not studied for 25 years, has been painted with red clay. "The riddle of the Red Deer Cave people gets even more challenging now: Just who were these mysterious stone age people? Why did they survive so late? And why only in tropical southwest China?" said Curnoe (leader of the research team).

—"Bone discovery suggests a mysterious ancient species of human lived alongside our ancestors" in *Quartz*, by Olivia Goldhill January 01, 2016, found at *http://qz.com/585000/bonediscoverysuggestsamysterio usancientspeciesofhumanlivedalongsideourancestors/*

Ung Strong Arm and Enga Dancing Flower had not gone far on their renewed search for Sooka before they both halted, stopped by an urgent summons sent out from Hama.

You must both return now. We are moving the village to the new location now. We need for you to help us move. After that, we will all help you find Sooka.

Enga screamed and fell to the ground. "Nasa, nasa, nasa!" She cried out the word for "no" as loudly as she could and pounded the earth with her fists.

My birth sister, Ung thought-spoke to her gently, catching one of her fists and stilling it. *Sooka is with Vala Golden Hair. She must be. We have never received any thoughts of distress from her. Vala is a person she knows, so she should not be in danger. It is doubtful that Vala will harm her.*

Enga shook her head. *Vala may not harm her on purpose, but Vala forgets to tend to her needs. She has never treated her right. Sooka should not be with her. Vala left her behind when she departed.*

This is all true, but I am saying to you that we can find her after we help our tribe to relocate. She will be unharmed until then. There are others there, the members of the Tall Ones tribe, not only Vala.

Enga was not convinced that Sooka would be safe, but could she defy her Hama?

Remember, Enga Dancing Flower, that Sooka came from the seed of a Tall One. That is why her thoughts do not transmit well. But it is also why she can probably communicate with Tall Ones better than a Hamapa can. She is not in a bad place right now if she is with Vala and among those Tall Ones. She will be all right for a while.

Enga thought that Ung was probably right, but it gave her such pain to interrupt her search once again. She felt that she might know where her baby was and that she was close by and that it would be easy to go and get her. But the tribe needed her and she must return to help with the move. It felt like something was cracking apart inside her, tearing her into two pieces. She would leave one piece of herself here, on this quest, as she returned to her tribe, until she could resume her search and reunite her two halves.

*****

Jeek was agitated, and almost angry. They were moving. Again. Would they never stop moving? Would they never find a place to live in this

New Land? He wished they had stayed in the Old Land. The Elders thought they would be killed if they stayed there, but maybe they would all die anyway. Why was this happening? Was it because their tribe had harbored members who did terrible things in the past? Some of them had killed other members of their own tribe. Did that anger the Spirits? Was Dakadaga so angry with the Hamapa that they would all perish, like the Gata and Yamapa tribes had? Was it any use to keep moving?

Could he tell the Spirits that not all Hamapa were like Vala Golden Hair? Most of them were not. But would the Spirits listen to him?

His fretting continued. He was unable to stop the worries. What did the Spirits think of him, now that he had also taken a life? He knew that he had taken the life of a person who would have slain him and others in his tribe, but he would never be able to forget that he had done that. He was not the person he had always thought he was. That person would not have been able to drive that spear into the soft neck of that attacker.

He found himself pacing back and forth just outside the village, trying to keep his thoughts and pain to himself. But Gunda approached and took his shoulders to stop him from taking another step. His thoughts had probably not leaked to her, but he could tell that his mood had. She could tell he was in distress. She always could. She stroked his arm until he felt more calm.

*****

It took two suns to get everything ready and to do the move. The distance was not far to the next new place, and they had done this same thing such a short time ago, which made everything more easy. Enga found herself being impatient with everything and everyone. Nothing was happening quickly enough for her. She was unhappy and grumpy most of the time, sending out sharp, spiky thoughts.

Hama agreed that she would let Enga take some brothers and sisters, as many as she wished, to get Sooka after they had moved all of their belongings to the most new place and were settled in there. That place would be more close to where they thought Sooka was, so the journey would not be long.

Thoughts of the death of Cabat the Thick were buried beneath concern for Sooka in the mind of Enga, but she was always aware of them. No one knew who had killed him. That killer could be one of them, as had happened in the past. If she raised the issue, the focus would move away from her quest to retrieve her child, though, so she did not let thoughts of Cabat come to the surface. She would do that later, though.

At last, on the third new sun after she had been called back, the move was complete. Enga had done her part, but could not sit around and enjoy this new place and all of the work she had done. She did not linger a moment more than she had to before she set off again to the place Bodd Blow Striker had described. The ones going with Enga Dancing Flower now were Ung Strong Arm, Fee Long Thrower, Tog Flint Shaper, and Bahg Swiftfeet. Before leaving, Enga tried to touch the mind of Bodd Blow Striker, but could not.

She asked around and found that no one knew where he was. Bahg said he had seen him walk out of this most new village early, at new sun, but did not know where he was going.

Enga wondered if he might want to stay by himself so that his thoughts did not reach Vala Golden Hair. She knew he feared that they were now too close to her, since this village was so much more close than the last one.

At the previous dark time, Enga had set the Aja Hama carving near the center fire at gathering time for them to dance around during the first night in this place. More and more of the Hamapa thought that the figure was a good thing to have and to revere. Also, more and more, they directed askings and sang thanks to Her. They had danced around Her before the horrid battle with the Mapa and they had succeeded in winning that day. If they danced around Her that night, maybe Enga Dancing Flower would find her missing child. They sang songs of thanks for finding this place and for reaching it without any more misfortunes.

The search party set out, supplied with skins of water and a few pieces of dried meat. They did not expect to be gone very long. Enga hoped Vala might want to get rid of Sooka by now. She had never liked caring for her. But, even though she could not tell exactly why, fear grew in Enga.

This day was not like the one, not long ago, when Enga had thought this place was becoming less hot. Even though Sister Sun had not been in Mother Sky for very long, she sent searing rays down upon them. Tikidoe had placed a lightweight piece of deer pelt on the head of Enga before they started out. Enga had laughed and taken it off. Tikidoe had put it back on. She pointed to Sister Sun after she did it. Now, as they trudged through the grasses with the heat growing, Enga put the pelt back on top of her head because it helped to keep her head cool in this too hot place.

Enga recalled the thought-picture of the location that Bodd had sent her much earlier, on her last trip to try to find Sooka. The Tall Ones were so close to this new place that it should not take long to get there. The route was clear in her mind. She led the small band toward that place with the appearance of more confidence and hope than she felt.

*****

Back at the new village, where things were still being arranged and set up, Jeek stood looking up at the mountain beside the village. They were dwelling on the opposite side of it now, having moved halfway around the huge hill. Now they were on the same side of the hill as the one where Sister Sun shed her first rays when she rose. They had found a cave on the other side, so he hoped they could find the same thing on this side, too. He thought he spotted a dark spot that was not very high up. They could get there with ease if it really was a cave. He summoned Gunda. *Would you go with me, to climb up there?*

She ran over from where she had just finished braiding the hair of her small sisters. He pointed, sending her a picture of the old Holy Cave they had left behind so long ago, then one of the caves they had recently found in this New Land.

Do you think we will find a good cave up there? she asked. *A place where we can birth babies, have first couplings? It would be good not to have to go around the mountain for that, to the cave we found back there.*

I do think so. Does that not look like a cave?

She squinted in the direction he was pointing, up the mountainside, a solid rocky wall high above steep slopes, illuminated by Sister Sun in the first half of the day. *We should go up and see it more close.*

Jeek smiled. He had been trying to touch the mind of Enga, to see how the quest for Sooka was going, but had not been able to. This would give him something different to think about. Something exciting. Then he would not worry so much about her.

Gunda caught this thought. *We are all thinking about her and about Sooka, and about the search party. It is not just you, Jeek. But there is nothing any of us can do to help from here. And we must stay and guard our village in case someone else wants this place, too.*

Jeek gave a mental shake at that. No, no, no, he thought to himself. No one could want this place, too. They had gone through too much.

He and Gunda walked in silent companionship toward the odd-looking mountain. The bottom part looked like a peak with a flat top. It looked like someone had set another small flat-topped mountain on the top of that bottom part. They started walking up, but the climb soon became steep, so they went one direction, then the other direction, making their way through the grasses that were studded with the prickly bushes that they had to watch out for, making a jagged trail, back and forth. They tried to stomp the growth down to mark the path so that they would be able to retrace their steps on the way back.

After Sister Sun had traveled the length of one hand, they sat to rest and sip water from the skins they carried. From where they were, they could look down on the new village.

We have climbed more high than I thought we had, Jeek thought-spoke. *That is good.*

From here, can you tell where the cave is, the one that you thought

142

you saw?

Jeek looked up, over his shoulder. He scanned the rocky terrain above them. Then he jumped to his feet. *Yes! There, see it?*

Gunda stood and looked where he pointed. *Maybe.*

Jeek thought Gunda looked hot and tired. *I can go the rest of the way if you want to wait here or go back down.*

She frowned at him. *I do not. I am not tired. We can go there together. It is not far.*

Indeed, it was not far. They went less than another hand length of Sister Sun before they came to the break in the wall he had detected. This part of the climb had been through rocks where only a few plants grew between them. There were some grasses, but not many. There were more of the prickly bushes. They bore different kinds of fruits. There were small berries the color of Mother Sky on some bushes, and others of a more dark color on bushes with thorns. These grew where Sister Sun could shed rays on them and they needed to be avoided so they would not stick into their skin. They both picked some berries from some of them and ate them. The berries were all ripe, and sweet and juicy.

The cave was much more large than it had looked from below. It was more wide than one Hamapa lying across it, but less wide than two. It was very much tall enough to stand up in. Even a Tall One would have trouble reaching the top of it with an outstretched hand. The back was in darkness. They could not tell how deep the cave was, but it was not small in that direction.

Jeek grew more and more excited as he spun around inside it. The floor of the cave was dry and the sides were not damp. That was good. They needed a dry cave. There was some evidence that others had lived here once, but that must have been a long time ago. Near the front of the cave, a wide area of the floor was charred, as if a large fire had been there. Around that, were some bones, one of them quite large. Jeek picked up a smaller one. The end had been broken off. When he looked at the other bones, the large one had also been broken. The smaller ones had teeth marks. It seemed to him that people had lived here and eaten the flesh of the animals these bones had come from.

A few small bats flew out, which made them duck, and then laugh at themselves.

If others lived here, he thought-spoke to Gunda, *we can surely use this space. It is not big enough for our village, but could be our new Holy Cave.*

Gunda was gazing at the walls of the cave. *These walls are smooth. I am having a happy thought.*

Jeek, curious, asked her what she was thinking.

We could put color on the walls. Draw pictures of things.

What made you think of that? Jeek had never heard of anything but stripes and shapes and handprints on the cave walls.

What makes me think of it is the Aja Hama figure that Enga uses, that was carved from a piece of wood, but it looks like a person. I have been trying to draw a person on the ground, in dirt.

You have? Jeek opened his eyes wide in surprise.

Gunda sent him a picture of a figure she had drawn. It did look like a person. It had a main body part, a head with some hair, two legs, and two arms. *How did you do that? I like it. Where is it?*

It is gone. My pictures do not stay in the dirt for a very long time. They disappear quickly. I do not mind. I have drawn them many times. The rain, people walking on them, those things make them disappear.

They you need to put them on this wall so that they do not go away. Jeek knew what she could use to do that. The Holy Cave in the Old Land had been decorated with red ochre streaks. He sent this thought-picture to Gunda.

Yes! That is what I want to do. To use this for my drawings.

I will tell the others of this cave now. He sent out a message to Akkal, the Fire Tender first, with a mental picture of it. *We have found a shelter where you can keep the fire.*

Akkal responded right away and sent back his approval. *Yes, it looks like a very good cave for us.*

Jeek then sent a mental depiction of the cave to the whole tribe.

Hama was pleased, as were the others. Their approval made Jeek feel a warm glow inside. A pleasant one, not like the one from a warm Sister Sun.

He and Gunda sat in the cave, enjoying their discovery and picturing the figures on the walls, for a long time.

Chapter 21

Emily Hallett, of the Max Planck Institute for the Science of Human History in Germany...in Contrebandiers Cave on Morocco's Atlantic Coast...found bones she wasn't expecting: dozens of tools carefully shaped, smoothed and polished into implements ideal for scraping hides clean to make leather, and scraping pelts to produce furs. "They look like the tools that people still use today to process hides for leather and fur," Hallett says. The researchers found 62 different bone tools in Middle Stone Age layers dated to 90,000 to 120,000 years ago.

Early modern humans and Neanderthals needed, and seem to have produced, clothing to survive in colder times and places like Ice Age Europe (15,000 to 70,000 years ago). But the climate around Contrebandiers Cave in Morocco was relatively mild 100,000 years ago, as it remains today... Humans might well have adopted clothing for comfort against the chill even when conditions were not extreme, adds Gilligan, an archaeologist at the University of Sydney who was not involved with the study.

—*Smithsonian Magazine*, September 16, 2021, by Brian Handwerk, Science Correspondent

Enga and the others who were trying to find Sooka knew that they were drawing near a settlement. They could smell people and could even hear speaking and other sounds, sounds of movement and activity. Enga even heard the high, light voices of children, but could not tell if one of them was Sooka or not.

Sister Sun was approaching Brother Earth, but had not yet gone inside him. She sent glowing rays across Mother Sky, catching on some of her cloud garments and turning them bright colors against the coming darkness.

These must be the Tall Ones we are looking for, Enga told the others. *They do not smell like us and they are making all those speaking sounds. That is what Tall Ones do.*

The others agreed. They always thought it was odd that the Tall Ones did not seem to exchange thoughts, only words that they spoke aloud. But that was their way. Not everyone was the same in appearance, thought or behavior. Even those who looked similar.

Should we wait for dark to enter their village?

Should we go now?

Should we wait for first sun?

Many thoughts flew back and forth. They all looked to Enga. *They think I am their leader,* she thought to herself. Maybe she was. She had asked them all to help her.

Let us sit here for a while and think about it. She wanted to see if she could detect the thoughts of Vala Golden Hair.

They sat in silence, wrapped in their own thoughts, all facing toward the village, in case anyone approached from there. The smoke from the fire the Tall Ones must have had rose and was visible to them. They heard children laughing and shouting. Their adult conversation sounded like buzzing. These were very noisy people.

Enga flinched when something touched her shoulder. She whipped around and saw that Tikidoe was standing behind her. She realized that the Hooden must have followed them. Her spirits rose on seeing her.

Enga jumped up and hugged her, so happy that she was with them.

This was just what they needed. Tikidoe would be able to tell them what some of those sounds meant. Enga gave her some thoughts, using lots of gestures, and made her understand that she was to interpret for them.

Tikidoe nodded to Enga and cocked her head to listen. After a pause, she started sending thoughts to Enga, which Enga relayed to the group, since Tikidoe had only learned one color for thoughts, a dark, private color.

They are saying that the meat they just ate was good. She paused to listen again.

Something else was good, too. Some other food. Tikidoe did not know that word for what they had eaten.

One person thinks her child is very smart. Another woman thinks her own child is much more smart. Another listening pause.

Their leader says they will not need to hunt for many days.

It sounded to Enga that these were all ordinary thoughts. She asked Tikidoe, *Can you find a Hamapa or a person who is part Hamapa there? Can you find Sooka?*

Tikidoe could not. She could not reach out to touch the thoughts of other Hamapas. She could only get thoughts from Enga, who had taught her. Enga was glad that she had succeeded with what she had done, at least. Tikidoe might learn to communicate with them all eventually, but she could not yet.

After a quick discussion, they all agreed to enter the village of the Tall Ones now and see if Vala or Sooka were there. The people in the village did not seem to be occupied with anything important.

They stood, stretching from having sat so long, and straightened their backs. Then they marched forward with Enga leading them. Darkness was starting to thicken, but the light of the village was clear in the distance and they headed toward that.

Before they reached the edge of the village, Enga kicked something with her foot and almost tripped. Tog rushed forward and caught her before she fell. They had been walking through a place where soft, tall grasses grew. Tog parted the long stalks of grass to see what Enga had stumbled into.

It was a person. It was Bodd Blow Striker. He lay in a puddle of Red. He had been slain.

*****

Jeek saw Pakk conferring in private with Hama. He could not read their thoughts, but he could read the smile on the face of Hama. Soon, she summoned the tribe so she could tell them something. A pelt lay on the ground near them.

We have not had time to process the skins from the last hunts, since we have been doing many other things. Pakk and Deeta have noticed the raw skins, the pelts from the hunts, that we have been carrying with us, and not using for anything yet. She nodded at the two Mapa.

Pakk and Deeta both reached into their waist pouches and pulled out small bones. They were smooth bones that had been polished so that they gleamed in the sunlight. They held them up proudly.

What are those? Jeek inquired. He admired the implements. They looked like they had taken a long time to make and polish, but he wondered if they were useful.

With these, Pakk thought-spoke, *we can scrape your hides.*

We already know how to do that, Gunda pointed out.

Hapa answered. *We do, and we use stone scrapers. We are able to clean the hides of fat and muscle and matter, but Pakk and Deeta say these tools will work better for that. And they have another purpose also.*

Deeta produced a small piece of leather from her pouch. *With this tool, I removed the hair from the skin to get a nice smooth piece of leather.*

The eyes of Jeek, and everyone else, grew wide. The leather material looked like it would be more cool than the hides they wore, hides with the hair of the mammoth still on them.

They have agreed to begin to process some of our skins for clothing, Hapa continued. *We can watch them, see how they do this, and learn how to make these tools so that we can do this for ourselves.*

Everyone was in agreement about that. Deeta passed around the small piece of smooth, hairless mammoth skin and they felt it, nodding and smiling.

Jeek paused while reaching for a piece, to touch it and examine the smoothness of it. He was receiving some thought waves from Enga. They were disturbing, but he could not tell what they were about. No pictures came with the troubled thoughts.

Chapter 22

Enga Dancing Flower and her friends stopped, frozen in shock. Bodd Blow Striker lay on the ground, not moving. The Red had flowed from his body. Much, much, so much Red. A deep, wide gash had opened up his neck. The tool Tog had made to chop down the trees lay next to him, as it had lain next to the body of Cabat. More Red covered the flint blade. The flint blade that was so very large and sharp. The most large one Tog had ever made. Enga knew that it must be the Red of Bodd that was on the blade, and that the blade had slain him. Bodd did not move, did not breathe.

The eyes of Enga squeezed shut. Had she been wrong to suppress her thoughts about the need to find the killer of Cabat? And to locate the missing weapon? Maybe Bodd would not now be slain with it, if she had made room for those concerns, or at least shared them with the leaders?

Tikidoe had been walking behind them, but she now came forward and saw the body of Bodd Blow Striker. She let out a loud screech and threw herself on top of him. Enga and Tog pulled her off. She was smeared with the Red that had flowed from Bodd.

Why had Bodd come here? How had that weapon gotten here? Who had killed him with it? The gash in the throat of Bodd was so very much like the gash in the throat of Cabat. To Enga, the gashes looked exactly the same.

The mind of Enga worked at a quick speed. The Red was not actually red now. It had dried and was more the color of mud. Bodd had not been slain recently. No wonder he did not breathe. Now she knew why she had not been able to reach his mind. She tried to summon up a list of people who would want to kill Bodd. His tribal brother, Fall Cape Maker had quarreled with him. They had disagreed on how to build the water crossing, how to move the log. Then Fall had scolded his brother for having stayed with Vala Golden Hair. They had both been angry with each other. But they were tribal brothers and had known each other for their whole lives, long before they came to join the Hamapa. And Fall was not here. If he had slain Bodd, he would have had to come here to do it, then return, without anyone noticing.

Who else would want Bodd to be dead? If Bodd had slain Cabat, the birth son of Cabat might want him dead. That son was Akkal, Firetender. But he was not here either. If he did this, he had come here and gone back without anyone noticing. The same weapon was used for both. Did the same person kill both of them?

Had a Tall One slain him? Would the Hamapa be safe with the Tall Ones?

Enga saw Ung Strong Arm lift her chin and grow tense. Fee Long Thrower, too, grew alert and squinted in the direction of the village of the Tall Ones. Then Enga drew in a breath. She smelled the approaching humans. Were they Tall Ones? Now she could see them. The shapes running toward them were, indeed, tall. They carried spears. They had to have heard the shrieks of Tikidoe. They were coming to see what was happening. Enga and the rest braced, in case the Tall Ones meant them harm.

*****

After the meal, Jeek sat waiting for the Saga. He looked forward very much to the dancing that would follow that, with Gunda dancing beside him. How was it that the skin of Gunda was so wonderful to touch? That her eyes were so deep and shining? That her hair was so silky? That all other females were less than Gunda?

He took a deep breath and realized that he was feeling a serene sense of relief. He had been feeling that for a time and it was growing with each moment. The new place was already beginning to seem like home. He had never wholly liked the first place in this New Land. Those woods behind it had always bothered him. Some thought they provided protection, but Jeek thought they contained the unknown. He had been proven correct. Those trees went on for a long way. No one had reached the end of them. Many strange creatures lived there, ones that he knew little about. Also people lived deep within the woods. Not all of those people were friendly. And the ones who attacked the Yamapa were hostile.

They were in the next place for such a short time, he did not think that anyone had had time to grow settled there.

The uneasiness that had consumed him, the fear that they would never find a place to live, was beginning to grow less. He thought that maybe this was the place they belonged. Maybe they could stay here. It was a good place. It seemed that no other tribes wanted this place.

There were many trees here, too, but the land was flat and it seemed more open. Also, there was the mountain beside them, its steep base rising close behind the settlement. It would offer protection that would be more complete than the dark woods. No one could come from inside the huge solid rock.

When he and Gunda had returned earlier and told everyone about the cave, Hama and Hapa had both beamed their approval at them. All of the tribe had been pleased they had such a good cave so close by. Now, as he sat in the glow of the approval of the tribe, he pictured, in his mind, what he and Gunda would draw on the walls. Maybe they would not both draw, but only Gunda would draw, and he would help her by supplying the materials for her. Akkal had told them he would carry fire up there at the next sun, so they would have a sheltered source for it in case rains came. It would soon be their new Holy Cave.

His thoughts were interrupted. Something was happening. Hama stood before them, stopping Mootak from giving the Saga. She raised her arms for attention. They all grew still. Then, in the silence, they all received what Hama had detected, the distress of the party hunting for

Sooka. Something was very wrong.

Jeek sought to enter the mind of Enga. He found such horror and fear that he almost drew back. But he felt he had to keep touching her mind. For a moment, the emotions blurred her thoughts. Then he saw it, what she was seeing. Everyone else did at the same time, too. Tog Flint Shaper, with just a bit less emotion, sent back a clear picture of Bodd Blow Striker, dead on the ground, with the axe beside him.

Hama sent a question to Tog Flint Shaper. *Does it look like he was killed in the same way that Cabat the Thick was slain? By the same tool?*

Yes, it does look like that. It looks like the tool I made to cut trees for the water crossing was used again.

Everyone else thought so, too, from the mental pictures they were receiving. But, Jeek wondered, how did that tool get here? Did Bodd kill Cabat and then take the tool away? Did he slay Cabat, then get killed with the same tool? Did someone else kill both of them with it? The wounds looked very much the same. He wanted to ask those questions. Hama turned to the ones who were here.

Yama, Yama Doe and Waid asked her what was going on, as did Pakk and Deeta, so Hama took the time to explain everything to all of them. They were not as fully attuned to the thoughts of those who were away, and they did not know everything that had been happening. When she finished, they were just as distraught as the rest of their adopted tribe at the kidnapping of Sooka and the deaths of Cabat and Bodd.

*****

The Tall Ones who had come to investigate the noise seemed as shocked as Enga and the rest of her tribe when they saw the body. One of them, probably their leader, came forward and started making those speech sounds, but no one understood him. Tikidoe was curled on the ground, sobbing.

Enga held her palm out to tell the Tall Ones to wait, and sat beside Tikidoe, stroking her hair and rubbing her back, until she became quiet. She explained to Tikidoe that they needed to know what the Tall Ones were saying. And that maybe they could help find out what had happened to Bodd. Tikidoe wiped the tears from her face with her sleeve and stood up. She and Enga faced the Tall Ones. The Tall Ones stared at the Red on the clothing of Tikidoe. Did they think she had slain him? But all of the Red was brown now. They should be able to see that he had been dead for some time. Enga held her arm to support Tikidoe, since she was unsteady on her feet and shaky.

Enga pointed to Tikidoe and to her mouth, then to the mouth of the Tall One. He seemed to understand that he should speak to the Hooden. Tikidoe concentrated while he spoke, then relayed his words to Enga in thought-speak.

They are sorry our brother has died.

Enga noticed that they knew he was their brother. Yes, he had lived with the Tall Ones, but they did not know Enga and those with her at that time. Maybe Bodd had described the tribe. Or Vala. Enga motioned for Tikidoe to continue.

They are saying that this person lived with them for a time with a female, and that both were from your tribe.

Enga grew excited. *Ask if the female is still there.*

Tikidoe made sounds to them and they answered. *Yes, she is in the village.*

Ask if she has a child with her.

Yes, they say that she has a small child and that the child is hers and is here with her.

Enga felt herself tense and she started shaking. She had taken her hand from the arm of Tikidoe, who now held Enga around the waist.

Enga Dancing Flower, Tog asked her, *what are they saying?* Enga had been shielding the exchange so she could concentrate.

Now she opened up and relayed this information to them and also to the rest of the tribe back in the village. There were some details to clear up, but Enga wanted to see Sooka as soon as she could. The Tall Ones, through Tikidoe, said the Hamapa were welcome to come into their village. It seemed that they said the body would be dealt with later.

Enga thought her own tribe should deal with it, but this was not the time to discuss that matter. It could be talked about later. Sooka was so near!

The Tall Ones had a low, private conversation, lagging behind as they approached the village. It was serious and earnest, Enga could tell. She kept glancing behind, wondering what they were discussing.

When they all got inside the ring of dwellings, Vala Golden Hair was sitting outside a structure and Sooka was playing nearby with some children of the Tall Ones. Before the Hamapa could do anything, the leader strode over to Vala and grabbed her by the arm, roughly. She squealed and tried to get out of his grip, but he held her tighter. She beat on his chest. Two other Tall Ones came to help, and one tied her hands together with strips of leather.

The Tall Ones must have been discussing the slaying of Bodd Blow Striker. Had they decided that Vala had killed him? How had they decided that? And what were they doing to her now?

It was probable that she had killed Bodd, Enga thought, but they seemed to be certain.

Enga could see how frightened she was, but none of the Hamapa tried to help her. Why would they? She had slain their own, tried to slay others, and they had banished her. They had all thought they would never see her again. They had not ever wanted to see her again.

However, the ones holding Vala stretched her on the ground, face down, her gleaming hair in her face. Then the leader took a tool that looked somewhat like the one Tog had made, the one lying beside Bodd, and raised it above his head.

Yes, they had decided she was the killer of Bodd. Enga realized he was going to cut her neck. He was going to slay her for punishment. Right there! She could not let Sooka see what was about to happen.

Chapter 23

The first man-made shelter was believed to have been made out of stones and tree branches. The stones were placed at the base of the structure to hold the branches in place. Man slowly learned to make simple tools that would allow them to build better structures, and later on these structures gradually evolved in shape and form. Other materials such as huge stone slabs, bones, and even animal hide were used to built [sic] the structures, which then provided much more stability, security and comfort.

—Found at *http://sheltertwc.weebly.com/history-and-evolution.html*

As early as 380,000 BCE, humans were constructing temporary wood huts. Other types of houses existed; these were more frequently campsites in caves or in the open air with little in the way of formal structure. The oldest examples are shelters within caves, followed by houses of wood, straw, and rock. A few examples exist of houses built out of bones.

—Found at
https://courses.lumenlearning.com/boundless-arthistory/chapter/the-paleolithic-period/

After a quick exchange of horrified thought, Enga Dancing Flower and Tog Flint Shaper, along with Ung Strong Arm and Fee Long Thrower, all rushed to Vala Golden Hair, positioning themselves around her and shielding her from the blows about to be struck. The Tall One lowered the axe to his side. He frowned at them, then spoke to Tikidoe.

Enga looked at Sooka, who was watching everything with deep concentration, a look of bewilderment on her small, soft face. She left the circle to scoop Sooka up into her arms and hold the face of the child to her breast so that she could not see anything more. Then she took up her position of defense again.

Tikidoe relayed the message from the Tall One holding the axe. *They know that this female killed your male. She brought that weapon here after she came here with the child. Also she wanted him to die. Now she has killed him. She should be put to death. Why do you not want to do that?*

Enga answered, through Tikidoe, hoping her meaning would get across. *That is not our way. We do not slay each other and she is one of our kind. We banished this female from our tribe and do not want her back. She was released to die, but we did not wish to be the ones to slay her. Nor for anyone else to slay her. Now, for this slaying of Bodd Blow Striker, she should be released, alone, and then she will die. That is our way.*

Also, Enga did not know that Vala had killed him. How could they know that? They were hasty people, swift to decide such an important thing.

It took a long time for Tikidoe to relay all of this. When she was finished, the Tall One frowned even more, wrinkling his large forehead and drawing his brows down over his dark eyes. He dropped the axe and pulled Vala up, then cut off the leather strips. Vala had squeezed her eyes shut when she was thrown to the ground. She did not seem to know what had just happened and she looked around with confusion. Had she been with these people long enough to expect to be put to death?

The leader spoke to Tikidoe, who related, *Tell this one that she must leave now. We do not want to see her again. She has fooled all of us. We are ashamed that we believed what she said about your male. This one—* he pointed to a nearby male—*saw her with the weapon. He says she left early today with it and came back without it.* Now he poked Vala in the chest. *Go. Never return.*

The messages all came through Tikidoe to Enga, then out to the Hamapa. Vala listened, standing with her shoulders hunched, looking small and afraid. Her cheeks were wet with her tears of self-pity and terror. Then, when the messages had been relayed, she straightened her back and tossed her hair back. After wiping her face with the back of her hand, she sneered at her own people and at the Tall Ones.

Yes, I killed Bodd Blow Striker. He was weak. It was easy.

She then walked with slowness, into the dark, carrying nothing.

At least we banish people with a knife, Enga thought to herself. *Vala Golden Hair will not live a very long while this time.*

She saw Sooka watching them. Sooka had lifted her head and followed the conversation, and now looked on as Vala walked away. Her eyes were shining with fear as she threw her arms around the neck of Enga. Sooka must have been afraid of Vala, or else Enga was sure she would have run to her as soon as she saw her. Now the body of Sooka shook with her sobs. Enga clutched Sooka more tightly and gave her a weak smile. It was the best smile she could do at this time. Enga rested her cheek on the top of her head and smelled her hair. The hair of Sooka smelled wonderful to Enga, but it was getting wet from the eyes of Enga. Sooka kept clutching Enga as hard as she could around the neck and they stood that way for a time.

A Tall One and Tikidoe had been conversing and now Tikidoe told Enga that this tribe invited them to stay in their village for the night. Tikidoe had also told them that Enga was the birth mother of Sooka. Enga had not even thought that far ahead, about leaving, or about what they would do next. Now she was grateful they would not have to try to be outside the ring of firelight during dark time. She nodded and gave another weak smile to the leader, who gestured toward one of their structures, inviting them to spend dark time inside.

Enga stared at the structure as she approached it. It was not a wipiti. There were heavy stones around the base, as a wipiti would have, but the rest of it was not the same. She put her head inside to inspect the dwelling. The wall supports were not constructed of mammoth tusks. They were made of wood, of logs standing upright. The wood was covered with animal hides, though, as was done for a wipiti. Such strange people these Tall Ones were.

She moved aside when others approached. Several of the Tall Ones ducked inside and removed some things. Enga thought they must be staying with another family so that she and her tribemates could stay. She nodded, trying to show them she was grateful.

They had taken some thick furs with them, a mixture of mammoth and large deerskins. They left plenty of them for the bedding of their guests. Enga thought it curious that, although their structures were so different, their bedding was very similar. The floor was strewn with thick grasses that rustled as they moved about inside.

After Enga crawled beneath a deerskin with Sooka at her side, she lay awake a long time, considering how these people lived. It was good that they were not hostile to her people. It was good to have friends who lived near. It was very good to hear Sooka breathing next to her and to smell her hair until she fell asleep.

*****

After the remote drama calmed down, Jeek had fallen asleep communicating with Gunda about going back to the cave and showing it to Akkal. He was glad his tribal sisters and brothers were safe, and that Sooka had been found, at last, and unharmed. The whole tribe had rejoiced at that. None of them wanted to discuss the fate of Vala Golden Hair. They had finished with her well before this. The dancing and the singing had all been about giving thanks and praise to the Spirits who watched over them.

At first sun, Jeek and Gunda were eager to climb up to the cave again, and to explore the area around it, to see what else was there. The others would not be back with Sooka until later.

It was a fine morning, very early. Sister Sun had not yet completely appeared and the daytime animals were just beginning to stir. Mother Sky blew a soft breath across the land. It was not yet as hot as it would be in a short time.

Akkal followed them, bearing his smoking burden of embers, carried in the large horn he kept for that purpose. He was a serious person, always concentrating on doing his job well. Jeek and Gunda had a private conversation, light and cheery, and Akkal walked behind them, wrapped in his own thoughts, whatever they were. Jeek never knew what he was thinking. Now, though, he knew he was most likely continuing to mourn the loss of his birth father. It was bad enough to lose someone from an accident or old age, but violent death was worse. Much worse. At least, they knew who had killed Cabat the Thick.

They reached the cave more quickly this time, since Jeek and Gunda now knew how to get there and exactly where it was. Sister Sun was shedding bright, sharp rays on them for the last part of the journey, and they were covered with their own moisture when they got there. After wiping off their faces with the edges of their garments, they all three ducked into the shade of the cave to cool off and to drink from their water skins.

Jeek and Gunda stood at the mouth of the cave, gazing out at a clear Mother Sky, who wore only thin wisps of cloud today. A carrion bird slowly circled in the distance, but they could hear other nearby birds calling to each other on the mountainside below them. They heard Akkal stirring and turned to see what he was doing.

Akkal looked around and tested the floor in several spots. He kicked at the blackened place where another people had built fires. It looked like they had built many fires here. There were some animal bones near that spot. Some of the bones looked like they had been broken off, some sawn off, and all of them bearing teeth marks where the meat had been eaten off. He moved farther back and started digging a shallow depression where he could deposit his own fire. This fire would stay dry in that location and would be able to keep burning, with occasional tending by Akkal. It would be the source of a new fire if the one in the village went out due to rain or wind. Akkal looked up, pleased, and gave a smile to both of his companions. He shoved the piles of bones to one side and prepared his pit.

Jeek watched him and sat, leaning against the smooth cave wall, glad that Akkal was so pleased. The wall felt cool. He closed his eyes for a moment. Then Gunda was shaking him to wake him up.

I fell sleep, he admitted. *I did not think I would do that.*

Jeek, Jeek, look! She pointed at the recesses of the cavern. Sister Sun was showing them how deep it was.

It is very large. That is good. Jeek got up and walked toward the back. There was plenty of room to walk around the fresh pit where the new fire now smoldered. The walls of the cave here were dark, but Sister Sun drew shining sparks from them. Jeek put his hand on the rock and realized that this part of the wall was made of obsidian. This was what Gunda was so excited about.

He jumped up and down and sent a brilliantly colored thought to Gunda and to the rest of the tribe. *The walls here are obsidian! We can have excellent new knives and cutting tools!*

He realized that even Tog Flint Shaper, who was away with the others, received the thought. Jeek could tell he was pleased. A shadow was passed with the pleasure. The shadow came from Tog and was because Bodd Blow Striker would have been happy to see this, also. He had been a skilled tool maker working with both flint and obsidian, as they both were. But Bodd would never be able to use this rock.

When Jeek came down from the mountain with Gunda and Akkal, Hama handed them some of the most tender meat from the last kill, cooked flesh with globules of delicious fat clinging to it. They were being rewarded for what they had done, guiding Akkal to the cave and discovering the obsidian. They had not eaten before setting out so early, so they were glad of the nourishment.

Gunda was the birth daughter of Hama and was expected to be the next Hama. Jeek tried not to think about that often, but now he did, as he sat beside her enjoying the meat.

She was the first born of the three female children of Hama and Hapa, who had been called Rho Lion Hunter and Donik Tree Trunk before they had become the leaders, upon the death of the old Hama, who had been the birth mother of Rho.

He started to think of the future. There had been a time, when he was more young, when he did that too often. He used to spend all of his time dreaming of things that had not happened. In recent times he tried to stop doing that so much, tried to keep his mind where it should be, on what was happening. Now, though, he let his imagination go wandering, and pictured things that might happen in the future, beginning with the ceremony where Gunda became Hama. He skipped the part about her becoming an adult first and having her Passage Ceremony, although that would happen very soon. In his mind, with these thoughts tightly cloaked in his own dark colors, Gunda was given the hollow gourd to rattle and get the attention of the tribe. Woven bracelets of hair, the kind that Hama wore, were slipped onto her arms. She wore a handsome cloak of new mammoth skin for the occasion.

Then he got to a part of the vision that made him smile and almost laugh out loud. He stood beside Gunda and was declared Hapa. He became the mate of Hama. He thought he might float up in the air and bump against Mother Sky.

Jeek, I am happy too. The thought of Gunda intruded upon his vision. This was the real Gunda. The young one, not the adult from his vision. He awoke from his daydreaming.

She had not seen his visions, but had felt his mood. That was a good thing. He did not want others to see those private thoughts. He acted like he was happy about their discoveries only and not about his dream. It was true, he was also happy about that. At this moment, Jeek was happy about everything.

Then the plight of those rescuing Sooka intruded into his thoughts. He wondered how they were faring.

Chapter 24

Capybaras…are the giants of the modern rodent world, weighing up to 100 pounds. [They] look like giant guinea pigs and have four semiwebbed toes on the front feet and three on the rear feet. [They] have a vestigial tail and are covered with long, coarse but sparse hair… Massive as they are, modern capybaras are only about two-thirds the size of the extinct Pinckney's capybara (*Neochoerus pinckneyi*). This rodent brute lived in North America from early to late Pleistocene time, perhaps 1.5 million to about 10,000 years ago… Paleo-Indians may have relished them, as people in South America enjoy extant capybaras today.

—*Ice Age Mammals of North America; a Guide to the Big, the Hairy, and the Bizarre*, by Ian M. Lange, p. 119

In the morning, Enga awoke inside the strange home in the village of the Tall Ones. When she first opened her eyes, she was disoriented in the unfamiliar place. Nothing looked right and nothing smelled right. The first thing she noticed was the smell. The skin she lay beneath did not smell like a Hamapa. The light did not come through the wall coverings the way it should in a wipiti. This was the dwelling of a Tall One family. Her mind came awake and remembered where she was.

And why.

Then she turned her head and saw that Ung and Fee were still with her, sleeping nearby. They, at least, smelled familiar. Sooka was also nestled beside her, which made the strange place feel perfect. She assumed that the rest who had traveled here with her, Tikidoe, Tog, and Bahg had arisen and left the dwelling already. Enga shook Ung and Fee to wake them. She picked up Sooka and they all emerged to find everyone else eating, finishing the morning meal. Sister Sun was well on her way across Mother Sky. They had stayed asleep for a very long time.

Tog patted the dirt next to where he sat, wanting her to sit with him, and gave her something made of grain when she joined him. She looked at it with curiosity. It smelled good. When she took a bite, it also tasted good. There was also a bit of tender meat. Enga did not know what animal it had come from, but it had a wonderful taste. She looked around for Tikidoe so she could thank the Tall Ones through her.

Tikidoe stood outside the circle of those still eating. She was conversing with one of the female Tall Ones. Enga sent her the thoughts of thankfulness. She saw Tikidoe nod, then speak to the Tall One with some gestures and the Tall One looked at Enga and smiled.

Sooka relished the food as much as she did, and seemed familiar with it. She had probably eaten this several times already during her stay.

Again, Enga thought about how relieved she was to find such a friendly tribe living near their new home.

As she was brushing the crumbs of the cooked grains from the tunics of Sooka and herself, Tikidoe approached. *I have something to tell you that is interesting.*

Enga nodded for her to continue.

These Tall Ones, who say they are called Tegyome, know of the tribe who killed the Yamapa back by the old village, the first one you had in this New Land. With the thought-word, Tegyome, came a picture of the earth. People of the Earth, Enga thought it must mean.

Are these, the Tegyome, friendly with them? Enga mentally tried to hear the sound of the name of this tribe. What a strange name.

No, they are not. They do not like them and they stay away from them. Those are called Gwehn, which means "killers," by the Tegyome. The female I spoke with just now, Dannah, told me that they are happy our tribe will be near and are also happy we are not living by the Gwehn any longer.

Enga relayed this information to the rest of her tribe and they gave the Tall Ones grateful looks. She wondered if the Hamapa might be able to trade with these people.

She asked Tikidoe one more thing. *What is this meat we have just eaten?*

Tikidoe answered, *I have asked Dannah that question. She says they are medium-sized animals that eat plants and have short ears and short tails. They feed in groups and are not difficult to catch.*

A pair of the Tall Ones walked by and Enga noticed their clothing. They were not wearing the skins of animals. They were wearing garments that were made of many small threads woven together. She thought she would like a garment like that.

Tog got the attention of Enga then and thought-spoke a concern to his whole tribe. *What are we to do with the body of Bodd Blow Striker?*

I think our tribe should decide that together, but they are not all here, Fee Long Thrower answered.

They had left the discussion open and Hama contributed her thoughts. *We banished Bodd and Vala once. But they did not disappear. They did not stay banished and did not perish. We did not ever expect to be dealing with the body of Bodd Blow Striker. I do not know what to do. Hapa does not have any good ideas either. Do the Tall Ones have any suggestions?*

Enga said she would ask, so she did, through Tikidoe again.

The Tegyome people conferred for a long time amongst themselves, speaking quietly. The Hamapa knew that the body could not be left where it was. It was too close to this living space and would only smell worse and worse, lying exposed under the hot sun every day. The odor was already evident from where they were. None of them knew, however, if the Tegyome could detect odors as the Hamapa could. They could certainly not detect thoughts very well. Maybe not at all.

Eventually, the Tegyome decided to carry the body away and leave it, much like the Hamapa did most of the time. Tikidoe told Enga that they would take care of it, since he had lived with them and the woman who also lived with them had killed him.

With much relief, Enga let everyone know that they would not have to deal with this problem. She decided that they would be coming home today, and bringing Sooka. That part of the trip had been most successful.

The Tall Ones even gave them a long piece of pelt so Tog could strap Sooka onto his back. She could not walk as fast as the rest of them, and they all were eager to return home with quickness.

As they left, the Tall Ones shouted out sounds that, Enga thought, were probably wishing them a good trip. The Hamapa made some sounds back, mostly "Aaaah" and "Eeee," trying to mimic the sounds, delivered with smiles and nods. They also mimicked the waving motion of the hands of the Tall Ones.

The trip back seemed more short than the trip they had made the day before. This time, they knew what they would find at the end of the brief journey. Coming here, they had not known what they would find, what would happen, or if Sooka would be found. They could not have imagined what they would find, Enga thought to herself.

She walked near to Tog and stroked the hair of Sooka often, giving her drinks from her water skin that had been filled just before they left. She put the piece of pelt, the one Tikidoe had given her, over the tender head of Sooka to guard against Sister Sun. When the rays grew too fierce for her, she put her cape on her own head. Her tribemates started doing the same with whatever they had with them.

At times, her tears blurred the path ahead. Some of them were for the sad life and death of Bodd. But they were mostly tears of relief and happiness, much like the gentle tears of Mother Sky on a warm day.

*****

At new sun, Jeek and Gunda answered many more questions about the new cave. They drew thought-pictures showing the size of it, the floor, the smooth walls, the color of the rock, the top—although they had not taken much notice of the top. Every time they portrayed the seam of obsidian near the rear of the cave, the tribe glowed with excitement. Obsidian was such an excellent material for cutting. It could be made more sharp than other rocks and was sturdy. And it was not found everywhere. However, there might be more nearby, since they had found this much in the cave.

Gunda sent a private message to Jeek. *Do you think a hole could be drilled in a small piece of obsidian? Do you think we could string some of it and wear it?*

Jeek drew a thought-picture of a bracelet, then a necklace, then some beads for weaving into hair.

They smiled and held hands, absorbed in their exercise.

But first, Gunda told him, *we must make sure there is enough for tools.*

Jeek was so proud of her. She was always thinking about the tribe. He knew this meant that she would make a good leader. He had never told her of his dream to be Hapa when she was Hama, but hoped she would think of that someday, herself.

Then he told her of an idea he had had during dark time. *Obsidian is found in other places sometimes, not just one. We knew where it was in the Old Land, and we also found some on the other side of this mountain when we first got here. I think the bones of the very large, very old animal that were at our first New Land village might be found more places also. Not just one place.*

The eyes of Gunda grew shiny and wide. *This is not that far from where the bones were. You are right. There might be more of them here. Should we dig and see if we can find them?*

We should, but not right here. We should look for them near the watering hole. The others were found by water.

Gunda nodded her agreement. They would take the flat tools that had been used for the water crossing, which they had brought along on the moves, and would begin digging near the watering hole. Soon.

*****

It was after high sun when everyone with Enga grew aware, as they trudged through the grasses on their way home, that an animal was near. It was not an animal they knew—it smelled very different. The animal was moving almost silently through the grasses beside them. The stalks and leaves of the undergrowth made noises as the hide brushed against it, but very faint noises. The Hamapa did not know if it would attack them or not, so they had weapons ready.

That is not one animal, it is a herd, Ung Strong Arm observed. Enga listened more closely and she could detect more brushing sounds also. Ung crouched low and crept toward them. Enga followed. She wanted to be with Ung if Ung got hurt. Sometimes Ung forgot to think of her own safety when she was on the hunt. And this was an unknown animal.

As they approached, the animals stopped moving forward. Soon, peering through the dense growth, they could see that the herd had stopped and was quietly grazing on the grasses and bushes. There were several of them, but not a lot, fewer than the number of fingers on two hands.

The creatures were large, more long than a Hamapa and surely must have been more heavy, too. They had sturdy bodies covered with coarse-looking hair, and heads that looked somewhat like those of peccaries, with small upright ears, but with short snouts. They did not have hard hoofs like those animals, but had bony toes ending in sharp claws. If they had tails, Ung and Enga could not see them. They were plump and looked like they would be good to eat. They were also large enough to have a lot of meat on them.

Ung Strong Arm, is this the creature we ate at the Tall One village?

Ung nodded to Enga and agreed that it might be. The rest of them thought so also.

Ung threw a spear and felled one. The rest of the animals rushed away as a group, moving quickly and making much noise.

The two sisters ran to the animal. The rest followed, Tog with Sooka on his back walking more slowly. Ung had gotten it in the neck and it was nearly dead.

Why did you do that, Ung? Now, what do we do with this animal? It is so heavy.

We can bring it home. We don't have far to go now.

Enga thought Ung should not have done this. It would make the rest of the journey more difficult. She was eager to get back and they were so close. The others also asked Ung why she had slain an animal now. Tog and Bahg grumbled that they would have to carry it. Tog took Sooka out of the sling and handed her to Ung, then the two males lifted the carcass, dead by now, onto a skin and dragged it.

If was fitting, Enga thought, that Ung carry the child. Maybe she should have been made to drag the carcass also. That, however, was a job for males.

They were not far away, though. Sister Sun was still up when they reached the village. They were greeted with joy that they made it back safely. Everyone wanted to see Sooka, and the small child ran from one to another, remembering them all. Enga hoped she would not miss Vala. She had not asked about her all day. Enga knew that, to Vala, Sooka had been a possession, her possession, to be reclaimed and owned. That was the way the mind of Vala worked. It was not a normal mind. Since Vala had left the Tegyome village in disgrace, it seemed that a long time has passed. It had not, but it felt like long ago.

When everyone had greeted them, Sannum Straight Hair noticed the skin the two males had dragged, with its heavy burden.

What did you bring us? He unwrapped the skin and looked inside. *What is this? It is a new animal, not one that we know. Not one that I know. Do you know what this is?*

It was nearly time to start roasting meat for the evening meal, so Hama drew her knife from her pouch and dug into the animal. After removing a small area of the skin, she extracted a piece of flesh and held it in the fire for some time.

I am sure now of what this is! Enga exclaimed when she smelled it cooking. *This is the meat that the Tegyome people gave to us. I thought that the animal looked like the mental pictures Tikidoe sent us. It will taste very good.* She took back all the thoughts of annoyance that she had had toward her birth sister for slaying the beast. It had been a good thing.

The animal was quickly butchered and pieces of it were cooked and eaten by everyone.

This animal is easy to catch, Ung told them. *We should try to find more of them.*

All agreed and were glad there was a delicious new source of food. Hama announced that they would have a celebration, to give thanks for bringing Sooka back to them. They would have it the next day, so they could all be prepared. There was enough of the new meat to have for another meal, and there would also be some extra to dry into jerky.

At dark time, after song and dance and much to eat, they were all tired. There would be a very large celebration at the next dark time, however. Now, weary, Enga and Tog put Sooka between them when they lay down for sleep. The child put her arms around the neck of Tog and rested her cheek on his, then did the same to Enga.

Sooka raised her head and looked at Enga before closing her eyes for sleep. *Where is the other mother? The one with the sunshine hair?*

The thoughts of Enga stalled in her mind. What should she tell her? Sooka had seen Vala banished, but must not understand what had happened. What should she tell her? She stuck as close to the truth as she could.

She has gone away. She has left us. You have only one mother now.

Enga could see Sooka pondering this. Soon, the child closed her eyes and her breathing slowed. Had that answer satisfied her? Enga would find out, when Sooka either kept asking, or did not keep asking about Vala.

Eventually, Enga, too, fell asleep.

Chapter 25

Jeek awoke in this wonderful new village, eager to dig by the watering place with Gunda to try to find more of the ancient large stone bones that might be in this place. He went out of the dwelling to get Gunda, but the first person he saw was his birth mother, Zhoo of Still Waters. She was standing next to Fall Cape Maker, who looked like he was in distress. Jeek had been able to tell that he was sad because his tribal brother had been slain in the last few sun times. Now he tuned into their conversation.

Fall thought-spoke to Zhoo, *It was not this bad when Bodd Blow Striker was banished. It was bad, because I knew that he had helped Vala Golden Hair do terrible things and I had never thought he could be like that. But, until now, I thought that he might still be alive.*

And he was alive. Zhoo put her hand on his shoulder. *Maybe you could sense that.*

Fall shook his head. *I do not think I could sense anything from him. I cut him off and he cut me off, but I would think about the time when we were alone, just two of us, when our own Gata tribe was gone, before we were rescued by your tribe. We were scared and alone, and we relied on each other. We trusted each other. I would not again rely on him for anything after I found he had done such bad things with Vala Golden Hair.*

So it is not good for you now. Jeek saw his mother touch her forehead to the forehead of Fall Cape Maker.

It is so sad now. He can never do anything to prove he is not such a bad person.

Jeek turned away from them and tuned out the conversation. He would find Gunda and they would dig up some of the stone bones. He would not think about Fall or about people who had been banished and who had died. Instead, he watched Pakk, using his tool to easily scrape the hair from a large pelt. The tool was sharp and worked very well. He and Deeta had already done several of the pelts they had been given.

Could he learn to do this to the hides, Jeek wondered?

Sometimes he wanted to do everything that everyone else did. He wanted to dig bones, to be a healer, to help paint cave walls, to be a tracker, to scrape hides, to throw spears. And to be a Hapa.

*****

Enga looked forward to the celebration all during sun time. She kept looking up and trying to will Sister Sun to move more quickly. That would never happen, she knew, but she kept trying it anyway.

She rebraided her hair into one long, thick strand down her back, pulling it over her shoulder to weave in shells that were strung on leather thongs. Some of them dangled so that they would make noise when she moved. She would not be able to wear a formal heavy fur because it was too warm, even at dark time, but she would wear a mammoth-skin cape for dancing. She did not always put on a cape, but it was fun to fling it, and to have it billow out when she twirled. Dancing was a place for movement and noise, and fun.

Sooka, come here. She summoned her child and braided small shells into her hair also. There was not time before the dark time to make a new animal skin garment for Sooka, but Enga brushed off the one the child had been wearing as well as she could. Eyeing the pelts that Pakk and Deeta were working on, she decided to ask for one someday.

The two, mother and adopted daughter, sat together for a time while Enga asked Sooka questions about her stay with the Tall Ones. She had not enjoyed anything so much in a long time, as she did being with Sooka right now. It was wonderful to have her child here again. Sooka chatted about the life she had had with the Tegyome, what they ate and how they cooked it.

Enga mentioned Sooka being away, and how much she had missed her, occasionally, trying to get the child to open up and tell her the whole story. No one yet knew what had happened when she disappeared.

Eventually, Sooka wanted to tell her about the night she was taken away. While Enga did not want her to have to think about it, she was glad the child wanted to tell the story. Maybe she could do it this once and it would be over. They could both put it completely out of their minds.

They sat just outside the wipiti where they spent their nights. The story Sooka told to Enga started with her recalling that, before she was taken, she had been playing at the edge of the village when she detected someone beyond the firelight. It was someone she knew, she said, so she went to her when she was beckoned. Sooka told Enga that she remembered Vala Golden Hair as soon as she saw her.

I used to live with her. She told me I was going to live with her again. So I walked away with her. I wanted to go back and get my toy. But she told me she would get me one that was better.

Enga was sad learning this because she knew the toy had not been brought along when they moved to the new village. It had been left where it had fallen, at the place where Sooka was taken. Maybe Tog could make her another one.

What did she get you? Enga asked. Sooka held her small wood carving of a bear now, keeping her grip on it as tight as she could. It was good that the toy had been brought along, but Enga knew Sooka liked the mammoth carving better.

Sooka stuck her lower lip out and pouted. *She did not give me this. I played with the fruit that falls from the trees with needles. Then a nice Tall One made this for me. I like it.*

So you went to that Tall One village then?

No, we had to do something first she said. Vala. She told me to call her Vala, but I know I used to call her Mama before I called you Mama.

Poor Sooka, Enga thought. She must have been confused. *What did you do?*

We did something else before we left our old village. It was not good.

Enga straightened her back a bit. She had wanted Sooka to tell the story, even if she was afraid of what Sooka would tell her next. The child continued, even though Sooka curled herself up to be small and scrunched her face so she would not cry. This was a hard thing for her to tell. Enga pulled her into her lap and stroked her soft, sweet-smelling hair.

There was a man in the dark. He was looking at some stones by the river. He picked up one and placed it next to another one.

The stone bones, Enga knew. She also knew who it was. *Sooka, you can stop now.*

No, I must tell you this. You must know this. Vala did not like to see the man. He asked her what she was doing and where she was going. He kept looking at me. He was from our tribe. I knew him. She told him that I was her baby. I am not a baby. The man stood up. I think he was called Thick. He reached for me and Vala put herself between me and the man. Then she picked up a piece of wood with a large stone tied to the tip. The stone was most sharp. She hit the man with it and pulled me by the arm. She hit him in the neck. He fell down. Then we ran for a while, and then walked for a while, until we got to the place where the Tall Ones are.

The first thought of Enga was that she was so sad her child had seen Cabat the Thick get killed. Her second thought was that they now knew for certain who had killed him. They would no longer have to worry about a killer being amongst them. Sooka had not mentioned that Vala took the tool with her. She could not have done that, since it was there when he was discovered later. Maybe Bodd had taken it. He might have done so. Unless Vala returned all the way back for it. The Tall Ones did say she brought it to their village, however that had happened.

She picked Sooka up and took her to Hama to repeat what she had told Enga.

*****

Jeek and Gunda had spent most of the day tramping out to the watering hole and digging with the wide pieces of wood in the soft, wet dirt there on the bank. They had not found any of the bones made of stone, but vowed to each other that they would continue to dig for them.

Jeek, there is another thing we should be doing.

He looked into her mind and agreed. *Yes, we should be finding some red rock so we can make pictures on the wall of the cave.*

She smiled at him. He loved it when she did that. *I have so many ideas.*

I want you to do all of the drawings, Gunda. I would not do them as well as you can. Your ideas are good and the cave will look beautiful with them on the walls.

They were walking back to the village, but their exchange was interrupted when they began receiving waves of excitement from the tribe.

Gunda stopped walking. *The celebration! I almost forgot about that.* She and Jeek began to run so they would not miss anything.

Sister Sun had met the edge of Brother Earth and was disappearing when they reentered the village. A huge feast was being laid out. Jeek and Gunda brushed the dirt from their hands and clothing and joined the crowd.

Most of them were bunched up, crowded around something or someone. Jeek and Gunda hurried over to see what was happening.

Pakk held out a strange piece of material to Jeek. *Here is yours. I hope it is not too big or too small.*

He saw it was a garment. Then he noticed the others were shedding their mammoth tunics and putting on the smooth, leather clothing. Deeta handed a similar garment to Gunda.

You have made all of these so quickly? Gunda asked.

Deeta answered. *We are not finished. There are a few now, though.*

Only half the people in the crowd were wearing the new clothing.

181

Jeek shrugged out of his mammoth skin and slipped the new one over his head. It was a plain piece of leather, scraped free of everything on both sides, with a hole cut for his head. He used the leather belt to tie it, the belt he had had for a long time, with his pouch slung on it. Immediately, he felt more cool. This was light. It did not weigh very much at all, compared to the heavy skin with fur on it. It would be a fine thing to wear in the heat, for protecting his skin against scratches and insects, at least part of it. His old mammoth skin would be needed for cold weather, though.

He joined the others in thanking Pakk and Deeta.

I am sorry we do not have one for each person yet, Pakk thought-spoke. *We will keep working until we do.*

Hama, who was wearing the new clothing, put one hand on the shoulder of Pakk and one on the shoulder of Deeta. *This is a wonderful thing. We are glad to have these. Thank you from the whole tribe.*

Jeek could not stop running his hands over the smooth surface of the leather as he ate. Gunda was also fascinated with the way it felt. They told each other how happy they were to have the two from the Mapa tribe with them.

It would make him even more happy if he were running his hands over the body of Gunda.

Chapter 26

The world's oldest works of art have been found in a cave on Spain's Costa del Sol, scientists believe. Six paintings of seals are at least 42,000 years old and are the only known artistic images created by Neanderthal man, experts claim.

Professor Jose Luis Sanchidrian, from the University of Cordoba, described the discovery as "an academic bombshell," as all previous art work has been attributed to *Homo sapiens*. The paintings were found in the Nerja Caves, 35 miles east of Malaga in the southern region of Andalusia. Spanish scientists sent organic residue found next to the paintings to Miami, where they were dated at being between 43,500 and 42,300 years old.

—by Tom Worden, 2/7/2012, found at *www.dailymail.co.uk/sciencetech/article-2097869/The-oldest-work-art-42-000-year-old-paintings-seals-Spanish-cave.html*

After everyone had had their fill of mammoth meat, the rest of the capybara, and some cakes that had been made of grains and fat and had been cooked over the fire, all eyes were on Sooka and Enga Dancing Flower while Lakala Rippling Water sent a Song of Thanks to Dakadaga for bringing Sooka back to them. Sooka beamed a wide smile the whole time, while the delicate tones of Lakala rose into the cool dark air.

Lakala also sent out a Song of Thanks for bringing the two garment makers, Pakk and Deeta, to their tribe. She gave thanks that they were still alive and could live with the Hamapa.

Enga was glad that the mood of Sooka had lifted after having to relate the terrible events of the night she was taken from them. The whole tribe had been told of it, but that was behind them now. They were finished dealing with that. She wanted never to think of it again. Maybe they would never know for sure whether Vala or Bodd had picked up the axe. But maybe, someday in the future, Enga would ask Sooka if that had happened, if Vala had returned and picked up the axe when she took Sooka to the village of the Tall Ones.

In their first place in this New Land, the rippling noises of the river would have been in the background of the singing, matching the tones of Lakala. Enga missed the sound of the water from that place, but it was the only thing she missed about it. Her foot tapped on the ground, ready to dance. She was also eager to get one of the new garments, but the Mapa brother and sister had not made one for her yet.

First, though, there would be the Saga. Mootak announced he would give them the Saga of Red Paint.

When Brother Earth was formed, there were rocks of many colors, but they were beneath the ground, under the skin of Brother Earth. They were pushed up when Brother Earth trembled. The rocks were very hot and it was a long time before they were cool enough to touch. At that time, our ancestors could see the colors. As they walked around among the new rocks, they touched each one. Some were the color of the darkness, some were the color of Sister Sun. Others were the color of water and earth. But when they touched the rocks of red, rocks that were the color of fire, they knew these were special. The red stayed on their hands. When they ground the red rocks to powder and mixed it with a bit of fat, they could make paint that would never disappear. They used the paint for many things, to decorate their faces, their Holy

Caves, and to give dignity to dead bodies being returned to Brother Earth.

Mootak paused and gave a nod to Jeek and Gunda.

I know that Jeek and Gunda are making special plans to use the red rock and the red paint. They will let you know when they are ready to tell you about these plans.

Enga smiled in the direction of those two. They both wore shy grins. She could see the surprised thoughts of Jeek. He had not suspected that Mootak knew of this, Enga thought. The plans must have been exciting, since they had leaked from Jeek and Gunda to Mootak. She hoped to find out soon what was going to happen. Trying to reach the mind of Jeek, she realized that that it was so full of other things, including Gunda, that she could not gain access to him. It made her happy to think about that.

Now Fall Cape Maker picked up his flute and Sannum Straight Hair began thumping a slow rhythm on his hollow drum. Enga took the carved Aja Hama figure from her pouch and set it near the center so that they would all dance around it.

Then Hama rose and raised her arms high. Enga grew excited. She was going to give a Pronouncement.

"Hoody, Hama vav," she intoned.

Listen, the Most High Female speaks.

"Hamamapapa ta Dakadaga. Hamamapapa aha baba Sooka."

The Hamapa tribe give thanks to the Mother Spirit of the Sky. The Hamamapapa celebrate baby Sooka.

Then she added something that made the heart of Enga grow even more warm and more full.

"Hamamapapa ta Aja Hama."

The Hamapa tribe give thanks to the Aja Hama.

The leader, as well as the rest of the tribe, were growing to revere the carved figure as much as Enga did. They could see that it might have power.

"Dakadaga sheesh Hamamapapa."

Mother Spirit of the Sky, Dakadaga, bless the Hamapa.
That was the signal for the dancing to begin.

*****

As Enga fell asleep at dark time with Sooka tucked between her and Tog, she went over the whole sad array of recent happenings in her mind. Maybe that would help to clear them from her thinking. She wanted those thoughts to leave her head, but they were not departing.

Such terrible things had happened. Soon after they had met the fellow tribe, the Yamapa, those people were nearly all slain by a tribe of Tall Ones from the forest. Bodd Blow Striker had reappeared, but had been killed. As had Cabat the Thick, who had been an Elder from a long, long time ago. The terrible Tall Ones from the forest had also frightened them all with the attack on her own tribe, but had not killed them as they had the Yamapa. The Hamapa themselves had even battled a fellow tribe, something no one could remember doing before that, not ever. But that tribe had not defeated the Hamapa. There was a good thing that came of that. Two of their members had taken refuge with the tribe of Enga. But they had lost too many tribe members in the last moon period. Ongu Small One was slain and Sannum Straight Hair was injured. The very worst thing for Enga had been when Sooka was missing and when Enga did not know if she would ever see her child again.

The mind of Enga pondered some more. Many good things had happened also. They had met new tribes, nearby, who were friendly. Some of the Yamapa survived and those people, Yama and Yama Doe and Waid, could teach them many things about their New Land. Adopting Tikidoe was another good thing. Tikidoe could communicate with the Tall Ones. They had even gained two more new people, the brother and sister, fleeing from the warring tribe. Those were Pakk and Deeta, birth brother and sister. The hunting was good in this place and they would not be hungry, as they had been before they left the Old Land. They had discovered the odd bones made of stone, the bones of huge animals. And Mootak, the Storyteller, had invented a new Saga all of his own for those bones, the Dragon Saga. Enga hoped he would invent many more like that one.

When she awoke and went outside, she did not feel as refreshed as she thought she should. The killings were resolved, they all knew who had done them. Sooka was back, and also the tribe was beginning to revere the Aja Hama as much as she did. Those were all good things. But something felt unsettled inside her. She did not feel she could relax and enjoy all the good things she had run through in her mind during dark time. She did not feel she could rejoice in any of it.

A gust of breath from Mother Sky stirred her hair, unbraided after the gathering. The breath that blew felt more cool than it had been. The days were also getting more short. Cold Season was coming. It would never be as cold as the place they had left so long ago, though. That was one more good thing. Why did she feel so odd?

She saw Gunda run to her mother, the Hama. When Enga listened in, she discovered that Gunda was having her Red flow. It was not her first, but she was wondering where to go for it, in this new place.

In their tribe, in the old village they had left many moons ago, a female went to the Holy Cave for the first Red flow, then to their own wipiti for other Red flows. Since they were now living with so many in each wipiti, that had not been possible, so the females had been marking off a space in one of them for females who were doing that. Most of them experienced this at the same time, all together, but not always. Gunda was having hers before any others had done so during this moon. Someone was always first, of course. Being in another new setup, the place to be private must be determined now.

Hama and Gunda disappeared inside one of the two large dwellings so Gunda could get settled. Enga thought about her own Red flow. When had she had her last one? With all the commotion of meeting new people, moving the tribe again, recovering Sooka, and even fighting a battle, she had not noticed. She reached out to the mind of Ung Strong Arm.

When was your last Red flow? Are you ready to have another one soon? She herself did not always have one for each moon cycle. Sometimes it did not come, but it would come the next time when that happened.

Yes, Enga Dancing Flower. Very soon. I can feel that it will be coming.

Did I not join the females when we had the last one?

I do not recall seeing you inside when I was there. I thought you might be having yours at a different time. Early or late.

No, she had not had it at a different time. She had not had it at all. If she did not have this one, it would be another missed cycle. Did she carry the seed of Tog Flint Shaper inside her again? Did she dare to feel happy? She was always aware that the last time she had carried a seed, she had lost it. That memory would never leave her.

Enga sat, staring at the fire pit where a few embers still glowed from the night before. She pondered what was going on, what was happening in her body.

Then she realized exactly why she felt different. It was because of a seed, a seed that would become a baby, planted and growing inside her. She suddenly remembered all the feelings from last time very well, at the beginning. There had been the many days of being sick, days of feeling tired, but such joy at what was going to happen. Except it did not happen. The sorrow that had come to her then had been heavy and deep. It had been a long time before she could push it aside in her mind, for even a moment.

Would she tell Tog yet, the one who planted the seed? She had to decide about that.

The decision was taken from her within one more sun. When she ran out of the wipiti early, just as Sister Sun was rising, and stumbled into the tall grasses to let her food come up, Tog followed her. Then he knew. Tog was very happy. He grabbed some grass stems and wiped the mess off her face, then stroked her hair off her sweating face. Enga had to return his huge smile because she also felt happy in that moment. So happy.

188

Chapter 27

Artists have been painting with ochre, a naturally occurring pigment, for hundreds of thousands of years. Their masterpieces range from prehistoric, ochre-pigmented images on cave walls to paintings on canvasses and other artwork from medieval times and onward…convincing evidence dates to about 250,000 years ago at the early Neanderthal site of Maastricht-Belvédère in the Netherlands, according to a 2012 study in the journal *PNAS*. The Neanderthals may have powdered the ochre and mixed it with water so that they could paint their skin or clothing… Archaeologists have found a number of other Neanderthal ochre paintings in caves.

—Laura Geggel November 20, 2018, in https://www.livescience.com/64138-ochre.html

Jeek saw Enga Dancing Flower emerge from the small wipiti. She had been having a private conversation with Hama. What had they talked about? He would like to know. He tried to touch the mind of Enga, but it was closed. He could not tell what her mood was, either. She did not look sad, but was not happy either. She was thinking very hard, he could tell. He knew Enga so well, but did not know what was happening with her right now. He could not help his curious nature and hoped he found out soon.

After Enga went into the woods, he saw Hama hang the mammoth tail in the doorway of one of the two large wipitis. When that happened it meant that some of the females having Red flow would be staying there together until that time was over. That must be where Gunda was, since he could not find her anywhere. She would emerge soon, within a few new suns, and they could climb to the cave together.

For now, this would be a time for him to go there alone, without Gunda. He knew what he would do with the opportunity. He hiked up to the cave and sat at the front, just inside it, for a few moments, looking out over the new village, which was still small, having only three wipitis. It would grow after the Cold Season. The fire of Akkal Firetender smoldered inside the overhang in safety, where it would not get wet, but where it would get enough air to stay alive. It was mostly smoke, but small flames danced now and then.

Arising, he walked to the wall of the cave and ran his hands over the smooth surface, picturing the drawings of Gunda on both sides of the cave, then strolled toward the back, deep into the cavity, where the obsidian gleamed in the dim, wavering flares of the fire.

It was now time for him to do what he had planned. He could not stand around admiring the cave for all of sun time. He left the cave and explored the mountain, looking for the special red rocks, and finding many of them. He tested a few on some light-colored rocks nearby, to make sure they were the kind that would make strong red marks on the wall. Besides, they colored his fingers when he touched them. That was how he knew for sure that they were the right kind. He filled his waist pouch and brought them to the cave. He put them in a pile, then went out and filled his pouch with them two more times. He stood in the cave and smiled at the nice big pile of red ochre rock he had collected. Gunda would be so pleased when she saw it.

Then he sat and let thoughts of their future First Coupling fill his mind. They would do that in this cave. They would be here, where he was now. He hoped these thoughts would come to be. He was having a good day.

The sound of someone approaching drew him out of his dreams. He quickly drew upon his own dark shade, the color of grapes, and made sure his thoughts were cloaked. He did not know if he would ever be Hapa, or if he would ever couple with Gunda. His thoughts were only of his hopes. They were very private thoughts. It would be shaming to him if someone read those thoughts and saw how he presumed he would be a leader. Leaders were selected, not dreamed into being.

Enga Dancing Flower appeared below him, on the track to the cave, a track that he and Gunda were treading and making more obvious every time they came up here. He jumped up, happy to see her, and watched as she climbed up to the cave entrance.

I am glad you are here, she thought-spoke to Jeek. *I was hoping you would be.*

If I were not here, you would have made this climb and would not find me. You could have reached out and found where I was.

I know I could. But I wanted to come up here anyway, whether you were here or were not here. I have sensed that you have been trying to communicate with me.

He hoped she had not been reaching out and seeing his thoughts. She did not act like she had. *Yes, I have been. Just to see what you are thinking about.*

She sat cross-legged at the front of the cave and Jeek sat beside here. *I like this place. This is where you can see so much below.*

Have you been here before? he asked her.

She nodded. *One time, but I did not stay long.*

They sat side by side in silence until Jeek was ready to burst. *Why did you hope to find me here? What do you want to talk about?* She must have a reason for seeking him out, but he could not imagine what it would be.

She did not give him any thoughts about anything for a few heartbeats. *I want to be with someone who knows me well, and that is you, Jeek. I am having a problem with something that happened.*

So, she did have important things on her mind. He had been right to think so. Jeek turned to look at Enga. She stared straight ahead. Then she opened up to him.

I have found that I am carrying the seed of Tog Fling Shaper.

Jeek was startled. He jumped up and hugged her. *We have not had enough babies in our tribe in recent times. That is so good. I am glad for you and for Tog.*

Then he noticed her body stayed stiff while he hugged her. She did not embrace him in return. She was not rejoicing, as he was. In his joy for the news, he needed to think why she was not rejoicing as he was. When he quieted his mind, he cast it back and thought he knew what her problem was. This thing was heavy on her mind. She was afraid. He could feel the fear in her, now that he sought it. *No, you are not going to lose this one. We are not on a trek. You are settled now and eating well and do not have to walk all day every day. You will not lose the seed. You will have this baby and it will live.*

He hugged her again and this time her body grew soft and she hugged him back. He felt that his check was wet with the water from her eyes. His eyes then gave forth the same wetness.

It was true that the tribe had not had many babies since they left the Old Land. Whim and Sooka were the only young ones and they had both been born many moons ago. There were not small babies now. They toddled around and babbled and played on their own.

Eventually, they both calmed and the fear lifted a bit from Enga. The friends both came down slowly from the cave with the mind of Enga a bit more lightened.

Just as they entered the central area, Fee Long Thrower disappeared inside the small wipiti where Hama was. Enga and Jeek separated, she to work on chewing and softening some new leather thongs that were strips left over from the cuttings of Pakk and Deeta, he to try to find a female who was not in the large wipiti.

To his surprise, he found not a single one at first, besides Enga Dancing Flower. He had brought a few small pieces of red rock in his pouch, down from the cave. He sat at the rocks surrounding the central fire pit and sharpened the colorful rocks to points so that Gunda could draw fine lines when her Red flow was over. While he was doing that, he started to put some ideas together. He knew that the Hama and Fee were not in the big wipiti, but in the small one. Enga was not in there because she was not having Red flow. She was carrying a seed for a baby. Were Fee and the Hama also carrying seeds? He grew eager for the evening assembly to find out if his thoughts were correct. Hapa would conduct the meeting if Hama were still confined.

Deeta, another female not with the rest, stood next to Sannum, with his hollow log drum next to them on the ground. Did she want to learn his rhythms? That would be a good thing. Sannum had a hard time drumming right now with his injured arm.

The two Yamapa females cast a shadow on the rocks he was working with. He realized they, too, were not in the tent with the others, as they stood over him.

Let me show you how we do this, Yama said. He could tell that this one was Yama from the red bracelet she wore. She drew a rather large clamshell and a round, gray rock from her pouch. The gray rock was stained with a red color. To his surprise, she took one of the smaller red rocks, put it inside the curve of the shell, then started to grind it with the round rock. She smiled at him as she produced a red powder. *We can mix this with a bit of fat or some water and it will serve as a paint that will last a long time.*

Jeek smiled and thanked her. He would look for his own shell in the water and find a round rock so he could make some good paint for Gunda with his very own tools. She should have sharp, pointed rocks that she could use to draw shapes, as she had shown him in the dirt, and she would also have the paint to color large areas, if she chose to do that. Her drawings would last a long time.

He wandered into the other large wipiti, the one housing mostly the males. Teek Bearclaw, his birth brother, was inside. Sitting very close to him was Tikidoe.

Ah, yes, there was one more female not with the rest of them. But she was not a Hamapa. Maybe her rhythms were not the same as his tribal sisters, as the Yamapa did not have the same rhythms either, it seemed. When they drew apart, he realized how close together they had been. Feeling like an intruder, Jeek soon left. He was smiling that Tikidoe and Teek were attracted to each other. He thought that was a good thing.

Chapter 28

Texas persimmon (*Diospyros texana*) is native to central and west Texas and southwest Oklahoma in the United States, and eastern Chihuahua, Coahuila, Nuevo León, and Tamaulipas in northeastern Mexico. The fruit of *D. texana* are black on the outside (as opposed to just on the inside as with the Mexican persimmon) subglobose berries with a diameter of 1.5–2.5 cm (5⁄8–1 in) ripen in August. The fleshy berries become edible when they turn dark purple or black, at which point they are sweet and can be eaten from the hand or made into pudding or custard.

—Wikipedia
https://en.wikipedia.org/wiki/Persimmon

The female tree produces a round, one-inch fruit that starts out green...but ripens to black by late July to September. To the human taste, the skin is bitter and should be removed before use.

—https://txmn.org/alamo/area-resources/natural-areas-and-linear-creekways-guide/texas-persimmon/

Jeek whiled away the time of most of the females being sequestered by doing chores, daydreaming, and observing what was going on with the new members of the tribe.

Since the new females were not doing female things at the same time as the Hamapa, Yama and Yama Doe and Deeta were outside during the sun times. The two new males, Waid from the Yamapa and Pakk from the Mapa, were becoming interested in those females. Jeek noticed Waid and Deeta sitting with their heads very close together having private conversations. He also saw Pakk bringing many things to Yama Doe, the former leader who wore the gold-colored bracelet. He mostly brought her things to eat and to drink.

One time, Yama Doe sighed and sent out a faint thought of being thirsty. Pakk quickly brought her a skinful of water, in his own water skin. He then offered to refill hers, which was empty. They left together for the watering spot and did not come back for some time. Pakk also foraged for berries in the woods and brought her handfuls of those, staining his palms dark, blue and purple, as he carried them.

Jeek wondered if Yama Doe was impressed by his efforts. He tried to determine if that was so, wanting to repeat the actions of Pakk for Gunda if they were working to his favor. When Gunda emerged from the wipiti of the Red flow, he would like to have something prepared for her. Something she would like and something that would surprise her.

Berries would not do. They did not stay good for very long, being easily crushed. Small berries were delicious, now that they were ripe, but they had to be eaten soon after being picked from the bushes.

He entered the woods, shuffling his feet on the ground, kicking at dead, dried vegetation, looking for something that would impress Gunda. He had noticed some small, twisted trees before, but had not stopped to inspect them. They did not grow to be much more tall than he was. The fruit was easy to get. Having lots of time right now, he reached up and picked the very dark, round fruit. It was small, easily fitting in the palm of his hand. He took a tentative bite, but had to spit it out because it was so bitter. His bite had taken the skin off part of the fruit, and the rest was juicy in his hand. It was making his hand sticky, so he stuck his tongue out to lick his hand, bracing for the bitter taste.

When the taste he got was sweet, he smiled. The inside of this fruit was very good. He picked two more, peeled off the skin, and ate the insides. Gunda would like these, he thought. He picked some more and stored them carefully in his pouch until the day when she would soon emerge. These fruits were more large and sturdy than berries, so they should stay good and fresh for some time.

Jeek felt a bit guilty about not sharing his discovery with everyone else, but he very much wanted Gunda to be the first person he told his discovery to. He wanted her to be impressed with him.

He had not eaten very many, but wondered if this was something that would make people sick. Reluctantly, because he wanted to keep his discovery secret, he went to Waid, who had lived in this land his whole life and asked him about this fruit. He did not want to give something to anyone that would make them sick.

That is a persimmon and they are very good, Waid told him. *They will not make you sick. I am glad there are trees nearby. We should gather them and tell everyone.*

Please wait. I want to surprise Gunda. After I do that, we can tell the whole tribe.

He thanked Waid for his help and bided his time.

Chapter 29

After a few suns, the females emerged from the large wipiti at first light. It had rained for two sun times and everyone was feeling restless. Jeek, hoping that they would come out that day, was very near to the door when Gunda stepped through it.

Come, he told her. *I have something exciting to show you.*

She beamed at him and hurried over to where he was waiting. He could tell she was glad to see him. He could also feel her trying to get into his thoughts to discover what the surprise was.

No, I will not tell you until I show you. He had his pouch full of persimmons with him, but wanted to do this in private. Privacy was sometimes a hard thing to get in the village where everyone could read your mind if you were not careful.

He drew her around behind the wipiti they had all just come out of and then opened his pouch. He reached into it and showed her the black fruit.

Is this something to eat? she asked.

It is. I do not think anyone else in our tribe has ever eaten it.

She reached for the small orb, but he told her to wait for a moment for him to prepare it. He drew his flint knife from his pouch and pulled it from the sheath of mammoth skin he kept it inside of. After he peeled the dark skin away, he held out the juicy, dripping ball to her.

She took it, tentative, but curious. When she touched it, she almost gave it back because it was so sticky. But he urged her to taste it.

Jeek! This tastes wonderful! Are you sure it will not make us sick? We do not know what this is, do we?

I checked with Waid. He knows this fruit.

They went back to the middle of the village and started telling everyone about the persimmons. Waid gave Jeek a big smile as he watched him gain the glory for another discovery. When he saw that, Jeek made sure to share the glory, telling everyone that Waid knew of this fruit and guided his discovery, which was only new to their tribe, but known to others. He saw Yama and Yama Doe, who must also know of this fruit, nod and smile at each other.

*****

When the other females came out, Enga was glad to see all of them. She thought that many minds were wrapped in some sort of expectation. She did not know why, since very few of them knew she carried the seed of Tog. Tog knew, and Jeek, and Hama. She had not even told Ung, her birth sister yet. For some reason, a reason that she did now know, she had not broadcast the news. Maybe because she feared she would lose it soon.

When Jeek and Gunda announced the discovery of the new fruit that grew very near, she tried one. How wonderful to have so many new foods in this land. Maybe it was not such a bad place to be.

That night, after the meal, Hama stood to make a Pronouncement, a solemn look on her face. She rattled her gourds toward the sky as her woven bracelets fell up her arms. Enga could feel the air of expectation, almost coloring the air around them as the air vibrated with the rattling of the gourds.

"Hoody!"

Listen!

Hama gave Enga a quick look, then continued.

"Yaya, Hama vav. Enga Bala Aha ah sema baba."

Yes, the Most High Female speaks. Enga Dancing Flower carries the seed of a baby.

Now the air grew even more charged. Every face turned toward

Enga, beaming at her, wrapping her in warm thoughts. She felt her shoulders lose their tension. The worried look she had carried to the meeting left her face and she smiled back. Now that everyone knew, it felt more right. More possible.

But Hama was not done. She raised the gourds and rattled them again, then spoke a second time.

"Fee Per Wegg ah sema baba."

Fee Long Thrower is carrying the seed of a baby.

Now the attention switched to Fee Long Thrower. The tribe could not sit still any longer. They jumped up and went to Enga and Fee, embracing them and patting them on the head. This was the best that Enga had felt in so long, even if her stomach was still a bit roiled. She knew that would last for a while and was not a bad thing.

A third time, Hama rattled the gourds for one more announcement. What could this be, they all wondered? This time she had a huge smile on her own face.

"Hama ad sema baba."

The Hama also carried the seed of a baby! The tribe members started jumping up and down, shouting and making loud, joyous noises. Enga had to stand up and shriek her joy also. There would be three new babies in the Hamapa tribe. Three new babies! This was just what the tribe needed.

It was almost too much to bear when Hama rattled the gourds for one last message. She told the tribe that Zhoo of Still Waters would mate with Fall Cape Maker as soon as the new Holy Cave was ready.

"Dakadaga sheesh Hamamapapa. Aja Hama sheesh Hamamapapa."

As Hama asked the two Spirits to bless the tribe, she nodded to Enga, who produced the small carved figure of the Aja Hama and placed it at the feet of Hama.

The singing and dancing went on for a long time, well into dark time. The seeds of the new babies were blessed by the dancing and music, as was the future new union, which would, it was hoped, also produce more seeds.

Chapter 30

Jeek sat very still, stunned after hearing the last Pronouncement. His own birth mother was taking a new mate. This was a good thing and he knew they were both happy in this decision. But he was shocked that he had not known this was a thing that was going to happen. He had been so wrapped up in his own doings that he had not noticed them becoming so close to each other. At least he knew about Teek and Tikidoe. That announcement would come someday, too, he knew. Someday soon, he hoped.

He would keep track of Pakk and Yama Doe. Also of Waid and Deeta. There might be a lot of First Couplings and new babies in this tribe.

For now, he danced with the others, pairing with his birth mother, then with Gunda, and then with the other females who bore seeds, as did everyone else. It was a joyous time and lasted long into the cool evening.

*****

After half of a moon cycle, and after much hard work traveling up and down the mountain, Jeek and Gunda were ready for the new cave to be revealed to everyone.

The day started with the whole tribe climbing to see the unusual markings Gunda had put on the wall with the paint created the way the Yamapa had showed him.

Look, there is a mammoth!

I see a wild boar.

Does everyone see that Hama has been drawn on the wall?

Jeek was so proud of Gunda that his grin was nearly as large as the width of his face. Gunda was more modest and merely smiled and nodded at the praise. Jeek thought that Hama looked as proud as he himself did, at the success of her offspring.

This was the last time so many males would be allowed in the cave. From this time, only Akkal, when he needed to fetch new fire, and a male who was using the cave for a First Coupling would be allowed there. Otherwise, only males who had not had their Passage Ceremonies would be permitted to be inside. Aside from that it would only be used, as was their custom, for the first Red flow of a female, a First Coupling, and for a birth, and those would be attended by many females, making sure the new mother was comfortable and had everything she needed.

Hama told them that the cave should be blessed now.

"Hoody! Hama vav. Dakadaga sheesh gara. Aja Hama sheesh gara."

Listen! Hama speaks. Dakadaga bless the cave. Aja Hama bless the cave.

It was now "gara sheesh," the Holy Cave, officially.

The hands of Gunda were still stained red from all of the work she had done and she gazed at them, proudly, her shy, proud smile not leaving her face.

After that, all of the tribe returned down the mountain for a day of celebration. A successful hunt had been made two suns ago and there was plenty to eat. The hunters had even caught another capybara. The breath of Mother Sky was growing more and more cool, which was a relief to the Hamapa, who were still not acclimated to such hot breath as they had felt since coming to the New Land.

A large meal was eaten, an older, familiar Saga was given, the cave blessing was repeated as the Pronouncement, a Song of Blessing was also sung to the cave, and then dancing began. One more extra blessing had been given to the union of Teek Bearclaw and Tikidoe. Those two now ascended to the cave, where soft skins had been laid for them, to have their First Coupling.

Theirs would be the second use of the Holy Cave for that purpose, as Zhoo of Still Waters and Fall Cape Maker had coupled there three days previous to this.

All would await the descent of Teek and Tikidoe after Sister Sun arose, and all would hope for another new Hamapa baby soon. This one would be half Hamapa and half Hooden, so they would not know what to expect, but they would welcome the baby and the tribe would love it and raise it. If the new baby was a female, they would train her as a Hamapa would be trained and they would see if she would be able to throw a spear like a Hamapa female. If not, maybe she would be a weaver, like her birth mother.

Jeek touched the mind of Enga and they both agreed that the New Land was a good place for the Hamapa.